OUR BROKEN PIECES

OUR BROKEN PIECES

SARAH WHITE

An Imprint of HarperCollinsPublishers

HarperTeen is an imprint of HarperCollins Publishers.

Our Broken Pieces
Copyright © 2017 by Sarah White
information address HarperCollins Children's Books, a division of
HarperCollins Publishers, 195 Broadway, New York, NY 10007.
www.epicreads.com

Library of Congress Control Number: 2016958063
ISBN 978-0-06-247313-4

Typography by Torborg Davern
17 18 19 20 21   PC/LSCH   10 9 8 7 6 5 4 3 2 1

First Edition

FOR DANIEL, JACOB, AND JOSHUA. FOR THE REST OF MY LIFE EVERYTHING IN SOME WAY WILL ALWAYS BE FOR YOU.

FOR ED SHEERAN. YOUR MUSIC IS THE SOUNDTRACK TO SO MANY OF MY STORIES—ESPECIALLY THIS ONE.

FOR THOSE WHO FIND THEMSELVES ON THAT INESCAPABLE ROLLER COASTER—AND FOR THE PEOPLE WHO CLIMB ON BESIDE THEM—LET'S RIDE THIS THING UNTIL WE OWN IT.

one

IT DOESN'T MATTER. I blow out a breath slowly, feeling it get caught on a hiccup before it escapes and rushes from my salty lips. The tears refuse to stop falling, even though I've had my eyes squeezed shut for at least five minutes. Seeing them together does this to me every time, but I'd rather hide in here than let them know. The cold of the tile in this disgusting old bathroom starts to seep through my sweatshirt and I lean forward, hugging my legs in front of me and trying once more to suck in a big breath.

I can't believe that as hard as I try to avoid the happy new couple, they seem to come walking down the hallway or popping out of a classroom when I least expect it. Leaning my head against the tile wall I attempt to block out the memory of my latest run-in with Brady and Elle. I thought I'd avoid their public display of affection by sneaking through the hall by the cafeteria to bio, and I was almost to safety when they came strolling out of the caf hand in hand.

It's been a long time since Brady looked at me the way he looks at Elle. His lips are curled up slightly and his eyes seem almost glossed over, as if he's staring down upon something amazing. I used to tell myself that he didn't look at me that way anymore because our relationship had moved on to something more serious. I could fool myself into believing that he wasn't enamored by me anymore because we both knew so much about each other. I realize now that there were lots of signs that he wasn't in love with me anymore, but I just wouldn't open my eyes up to see them. It didn't help that the one time I had voiced my concerns about Brady's behavior my best friend had told me it was all in my head.

Elle and I met on our first day of kindergarten. Her ponytail got caught in the zipper of her backpack and I had to walk her to the office. I spent the entire time telling jokes to distract her from the possibility that the principal was going to have to cut her ponytail off, and by the time we made it down the hall we were already planning our first playdate. We'd been best friends ever since. When we were little we had a standing Friday night sleepover, just the two of us, and when we were older we always got ready for a party at one of our houses. I was the first person she told when her parents were getting a divorce and she was the person I went to when my grandmother was diagnosed with cancer. I called her the second I got home from the date where Brady said he loved me. I really could have used her friendship when I needed to tell someone about how he'd broken my heart.

The betrayal came out of nowhere. If I didn't see it for myself, I would have never believed that either of them was capable of hurting me so deeply. I still wonder what it might be like if I hadn't left my sweatshirt in my car that morning two weeks ago. I only had ten minutes before the first bell rang, but I wouldn't get another chance to grab it until lunch. Brady's truck was parked a few spots down from mine and I could hear his music blaring through the open windows, so after grabbing my sweatshirt, I headed to his truck and peeked into the open window assuming I'd find him gathering his football gear. Instead, I found him making out with my best friend.

Remembering that moment in the parking lot still turns my stomach. It's not even like they were trying to be stealth about it. Anyone running a little late would have seen them out there together. I stood there, speechless, as I watched the two of them throw away years of friendship in the back seat of his truck. I don't even remember what I said that got their attention, but I remember running back to my car on legs that felt boneless. It felt like I was watching it play out in a movie—my body completely disconnected from my mind. By the time I pulled into my driveway at home after school, my brain was swimming with a million questions about how long it had been going on and who might have known.

If someone had tried to tell me a few weeks ago that I'd be running from a problem, I wouldn't have believed them. As a matter of fact, no one would have believed it. I'm the girl who people always say has everything together. Before the breakup, I'd never cried at school or behaved in any way that would make people think I had any problem bigger than trying to get my parents to extend my curfew. That obviously wasn't true—but no one but Elle knew that. Now, though, I don't think any of my classmates would see me crying on the bathroom floor and think that I had my life together.

I hear the next bell, letting me know I'm late for fifth period, but it doesn't matter. I'm not going to any more classes today. I just want to wait in here until I know that everyone has cleared the halls, and then I'm going to the nurse's office to complain of a stomachache. I know that it's actually supposed to be good if I see Elle and Brady. If I see them together often enough I will eventually get used to the sight and I won't feel like curling up in a ball. I want to believe that, but my heart still burns and my stomach tosses every time it happens. I've seen them together a dozen times and I haven't noticed any reduction in the intensity of the pain it causes me.

The nurse buys my story and puts me on the phone with my mom. She sighs heavily into the phone. "Are you seeing Laura today?"

"Yes, at four."

"Okay, put the nurse back on, but promise me you'll talk to Laura about this. I'm worried about you. You made a commitment to volunteer at the retirement home and I know you haven't been going. You haven't been out for a run in a while, you're not calling any friends, and now you're missing school." I hear my mom's receptionist in the background, letting her know her next patient has arrived.

"I promise." She didn't even have to ask, I would be telling Laura all about it on my own. Maybe she would have some great secret she could teach me that would help me hold it together when I see Brady and Elle. Inside I still want to be that girl who laughs in the hallway with her friends; I'd even settle for being the girl who got panic attacks because of stress over things like my AP classes and filling out applications, like I was earlier this year.

The nurse signs my off-campus pass and I head straight

for my car. My appointment with Laura isn't for another two hours, but I decide to go early and read. Her office is in an old building and the waiting room is shared with a few of the other therapists. It's one of my favorite places to be now because no one there expects me to be okay. For two weeks now it's felt like my family is collectively holding their breath. Everyone is waiting for me to put this whole experience behind me and I hate the idea that I am disappointing them by not getting over it faster.

The first time I found myself on Laura's couch, I didn't want to talk to her. I was a little embarrassed that I couldn't handle the panic attacks on my own. My mom thought it would be helpful if I had someone I could talk to every week. I didn't expect to like her so much, but somewhere between the moment my mom stood up to leave us alone and the scratching of Laura's pen in her outdated planner as we made another appointment, I decided she was all right.

As I drive to Laura's office I can't help thinking about how Los Angeles can feel so big, stretching along the coast for miles and miles, and yet somehow it is impossible to go anywhere without being reminded of Brady and Elle and the fun we had together. Proving my point, I notice that I'm passing the burger stand where Brady took me on our first date. I'd been so excited when he asked me out. We were seat partners in science class our sophomore year and while we'd flirted during every lab, I had no idea that he ever wanted our relationship to go beyond that. By the end of the first semester though we were a perfect high-school-sweetheart couple. We'd been back to the burger stand only a couple weeks ago to celebrate that we'd both gotten into UCLA.

I do my best to tuck away that memory as I pull into Laura's parking lot. I leave my backpack in the car but take my book and head for the comforting quiet of the large reception area. My favorite spot on the couch is open, and I throw my book down to save the seat before grabbing the key to the bathroom that hangs on the wall by the front desk. If I wait any longer the two-stall bathroom might get crowded with people as they finish their appointments. As I walk down the hall I hear my phone chime with a text.

HEATHER: Elle told me what you really think of me. I can't believe I trusted you.

I feel a knot form in my stomach as I read Heather's message. This sort of thing has been happening to me all week. Elle and I had so many years of friendship between us that we told each other everything. I thought I could trust her even if we got into an argument, but I'm learning quickly that she won't keep my secrets to herself if it means getting our friends to pick her side.

Heather has always been that friend who acts like her sole purpose in life is to have a good time. When she wasn't throwing parties at her parents' house she was persuading all the girls in our group to make a midnight run to the In-N-Out drive-through. And while we weren't super close, we'd always gotten along. I don't know what Elle could have possibly told her, but there are two things I'm certain of: 1) it was probably an offhand comment that in no way represented how I felt about her and 2) it's not good.

ME: Heather I don't know what you're talking about.

HEATHER: If you thought I was nosy you should have just told me yourself.

ME: I don't remember calling you nosy. And I would never want to hurt your feelings. But it's not like you've never messed up before. I mean, you knew about Elle and Brady and you didn't tell me.

HEATHER: It wasn't any of my business! Besides I'm better friends with Elle than you.

I stare at my cell screen for a moment, torn between rage and sadness. The fact that so many of my friends knew about Brady and Elle before me still really hurts. Not only did none of them tell me that it was going on, but now that Brady and Elle have officially started dating, all of our mutual friends expect me to act like what they did is totally okay. It doesn't exactly give me warm and fuzzy feelings about my friends when I realize they care more about making sure things stay pleasant than how I'm actually feeling. I tuck my phone back into my pocket and unlock the bathroom door.

The mirror above the sink is cracked, but it doesn't hide the fact that I look worn down and miserable. I wet a paper towel and wipe my face, letting the cold towel sit on my eyes for a minute before I toss it in the trash. My long brown hair is a tangled mess from driving with my windows down and even though I know Laura won't care, I try to brush it out with my fingers the best I can.

The waiting room is empty when I take a seat on the low couch and flip to my place in my book. I'm trying hard to focus on the story, but my thoughts keep drifting and I have to start the page all over. The music in the room is a soft jazz, the kind you only hear in waiting rooms, elevators, and doctors' offices. My eyes feel heavy and I give in to closing them, resting my head on the armrest and curling my feet up underneath me.

two

THE SOUND OF someone pushing open the heavy glass door startles me and I open my tired eyes and try to remember where I am. I must have fallen asleep because now the waiting room is crowded and the only spot left is the space next to me on the couch. I figure this out right about the same time the new arrival does, and I sit up straight, putting my feet back on the ground so he can sit comfortably. The boy looks familiar but I can't quite place him. His dark hair is cut very short, like Brady wears his for football, and his face is clean shaven. What really stands out, though, are his unusual multicolored irises.

I quickly turn my head so I'm not staring, and he sits down beside me, the scent of men's soap drifting past me as he gets comfortable. He's wearing jeans that hang a little from his hips and a black hoodie. I also notice he has on flip-flops and for some reason that makes me smile. He's holding a spiral notebook on his lap and I chance a quick look at his face again, curious about all the colors in those unusual eyes—the ones I find looking back at me a second before he looks away.

I've never actually seen anyone my age in the waiting room before. I know that plenty of other teenagers see therapists, but sometimes it feels like I am the only one my age who actually goes to one. I wonder what the boy's story is and whether it is anything like mine. I try not to look at him as he pulls a cell phone from his pocket and checks the time: 3:50. I must have been sleeping really soundly. The door to Laura's office opens and a mom with a baby on her hip makes arrangements to meet with her again. "One minute," Laura mouths to me and I nod my head. The woman and baby leave and Laura's door shuts.

I wonder if she saw me out here sleeping. How embarrassing. I take a deep breath again, catching a hint of the boy's fresh scent. The faint smell of chlorine has me intrigued—maybe he's a swimmer or a pool cleaner. One of the reasons why I got into volunteering and peer mediation is that I love talking to new people and finding out about their lives. It's probably why I'm almost tempted to ask him about it, but I don't know what the rules are here—not the actual rules, I'm sure I'm fine there, but the unwritten ones. Is it okay to talk to another person while you wait for your therapist? While they wait for theirs? What's he here for?

I know that looks can be deceiving, but he seems fine. He smiled, even. There are probably a million reasons why someone would go to therapy. I don't get much of a chance to really think about it though before Laura steps out of her office again and motions for me to come in. I stand up and take a few steps in her direction, but stop short when I hear a low voice call to me from the couch.

"Everly, you forgot your book." I turn and watch the boy close the distance between us and hand me the tattered paperback I'd left next to the couch. He looks down to the cover and smiles. I open my mouth to say something, but the door next to us opens and an older man steps out.

"Gabe, are you ready?" He looks right at my cute boy—not *my* cute boy, *the* cute boy. With a slight smile Gabe lets go of my book and slips inside the office of the gray-haired man, closing the door behind him.

"I'm sorry, Everly," Laura says as I move around a few of the pillows on her couch. I grab one and hold it in front of me to give my hands something to do. "That boy knew your name. We can switch your appointment time if you want more privacy. I try to make sure I don't book kids the same age back-to-back to avoid awkward waiting room run-ins, but I can't control the other therapists' calendars."

"That's okay," I assure her. "I don't know him. Maybe he knows me because of my sister or something." If he went to my school I would have noticed him before, wouldn't I?

"If you're sure." She looks at me carefully like she might have the power to see if I'm lying.

"I'm sure. He might not be here for therapy every week like I am. Probably won't see him again." I wonder if she will give me a little more information, like maybe that she's seen him here before or that he always comes here on Mondays so him being here today was a surprise. My therapy appointments are always on Tuesday. Instead she just shrugs and then sits down in her high-backed chair.

"How has the week been?" She looks at me empathetically and I answer her with a slight lift of my shoulders.

"As horrible as I expected."

"Anything new happen since we talked last?"

"I sort of lost it again today." I pick at a feather that's escaping the pillow on my lap through the fabric. "I saw him holding her hand and I just froze. A poor freshman behind me bumped right into my back and dropped all of his books. I couldn't even help him pick them up. As soon as my brain figured out I was standing in the middle of the walkway staring at their stupid hands I burst into tears and hid in the bathroom." I feel the embarrassment of the whole experience again, but surprisingly the tears don't flow. Maybe I'm finally all out of them.

"Remember the chart I talked to you about last time? I told you we would work on it this week and I'd want you to take it home for homework?" She reaches for a fresh sheet of paper from the notebook on the desk. She hands it to me on a plastic clipboard and then digs around for a pen in her desk.

"I remember," I answer as I watch her move around the contents of her drawer. She seems so put together, but small moments like this make her seem more human.

She finally tosses a pen at me. "I want us to start with what happened today. Make four columns. Title the first one *Situation*." I do as she asks and then wait for her next instruction.

"Write down what happened. Not all the details, just the part that hurt the most." She waits patiently while I write *Brady held Elle's hand*. "Now title the next column *Feelings*. Write down what you felt. Note if you felt sad or if your stomach ached." She waits again and this time I take a minute to think about my answer.

I write *sad, hurt, devastated*. Then below that I write

stomachache, headache, heartache. Laura peeks at my paper and then nods her head. "Title the next column *Unhelpful Thought*. Write down the thought that hurt you."

"I don't know the thought. I just saw them and then lost it." I hold the pen above the paper and feel the roll of my stomach again just from replaying the situation.

"Take your time." I know this means that I'm not getting off the hook. I think about being in the hallway and watching him take her hand as if he'd been doing it for years. I let the tip of the pen slide along the paper as I write, *It should be my hand. He doesn't love me anymore. I'm not his anymore. He is not mine*. Then I save her the trouble of peeking by reading what I wrote.

"Now title the last column *Alternative Thought*. Let's see if we can reframe some of those negative thoughts and come up with some more helpful ones."

I move the pillow out from between my body and the clipboard. "I don't know what to write."

"Let's start with the first unhelpful thought, 'It should be my hand.' What's an alternative thought to that? Remember last time we talked about not using the word *should*." My mind is still blank. I can't think of one thought that erases the pain of the thought on the paper in front of me. I'm used to being a good student, so I feel this pressure to answer her and give her the right response.

"Um, I guess at least I got to hold his hand?" It sounds more like a question than an answer, but she smiles at me and gives me a little nod.

"That's a good start. This will get easier. Let's move on to 'He doesn't love me anymore.' What evidence do you have that that's true?"

"He's with her. He was talking to her when we were still together. He doesn't care that it hurt me or that my life feels like it's been turned upside down. He doesn't care that I'm embarrassed at school because everyone knew except me." I reach for the tissues on the ottoman between us.

"It's not possible to love two people at once? Being with her means he doesn't love you?" She waits for her words to sink in and then continues, "He's told you he doesn't care that it hurt you? I thought he was visibly sad when you confronted him about her. Could those feelings be gone already after only two weeks?"

She's right of course. It's possible to love two people at once, but why does he have to love her? Maybe it isn't even love yet. Maybe he just really likes her. "He was upset when I found them. He told me he didn't want to hurt me. His actions just said otherwise."

"Okay. So what I've heard is that he still cares about you. It might not be in the way you want, but he cares. He told you he didn't want to hurt you. His actions were painful, but it's possible he was trying not to hurt you, just really messing that up." She smiles at me and I smile back.

"He really messed that up."

"How are things with Elle this week?"

I let out a big sigh and take my phone out of my pocket to show her the texts from Heather. "I've had three different girls confront me about something she told them I said. I don't get it. Why does she have to keep doing it to me?"

"There's a saying in recovery, 'Keep your side of the street clean.' It means don't worry about what other people are doing and why they are doing it. Just do what's right on your side and let the universe take care of the rest." Laura spins her pen once in her fingers. I watch it closely, letting her words sink in.

"So you're saying I shouldn't defend myself or attack Elle?"

With a few nods Laura answers, "If you said mean things, apologize. Everyone makes mistakes. If you tell others what Elle told you, you are no better than she is and what would it prove? It would only hurt those people to hear her opinion. Just let it go and be the bigger person. Eventually all this drama will stop." She sets the folders aside and reaches for her appointment book. "I want to start working on your staircase of fear. We will work on conquering your fears one step at a time until the biggest fear doesn't feel so overwhelming anymore. Be thinking about what those fears might be."

The hour is up so we book another appointment for next week. She offers me a different time in case I want to try to avoid the boy from the waiting room, but I tell her I'll keep my usual spot. I've been coming here for two years already and this is the first time I've ever seen him, so it's entirely possible he won't be here next week.

I notice he's not in the waiting room as I make my way toward the exit. The office he disappeared into is closed and there are only a few people in the waiting room. I open the heavy glass door and then make my way down the steps and out to the parking lot to my car. I slip inside and pull out of my spot.

As I push the preset buttons on my radio until I find a song I don't hate—no one tells you that being dumped will ruin every love song ever written—I notice the big truck in front of me waiting for an opening in traffic so it can pull out onto the busy street. My eyes flick up to the driver's-side mirror and I can see the boy from the waiting room in its reflection. I watch in the mirror as he rubs his head, then rests his arm just outside the window. His gaze falls down to the mirror and our eyes lock.

He doesn't look away immediately. I see him smile slightly and then his eyes return to the road. When there is a break in the traffic he turns left, lifting his hand in a good-bye wave as I watch his truck pull across the traffic lanes and then disappear around a bend in the road.

three

I'M WATCHING AN episode of one of my favorite shows I've downloaded on my computer and trying to come up with ideas for our school's spirit week when I hear my sister Rosie's footsteps zooming up the stairs and falling heavy on the carpet just outside my door. I glance down at the calendar in front of me and try to look busy when she opens my door without knocking. "Hey," she says, a little breathless from her rapid ascent of the stairs.

"Hey." I look up for a second at her pink cheeks, flushed from the sun and her exertion. I'm envious of her not for the first time in my life. Even though she is two years younger than me my sister has always been a force to be reckoned with.

"Feel like doing anything?" she asks.

"What do you have in mind?" I ask, pushing aside my schoolbooks to make room for her on my bed. I don't feel like doing anything, but I also don't want to give her reason to think she should talk to Mom about my disinterest in all activities. She smiles and bounces over, folding her legs so she's perched right next to me. I push up off my stomach and mimic her pose. My body is sore, punishing me from staying in one place too long.

"We could share a Special C from El Burrito Jr." El Burrito Jr. has been around since before we were born and everyone refers to their items as letters around here, most people having at least the first ten memorized. Our favorite thing to get is the two bean-and-cheese burritos and a soda special. Once a weekly stop, I haven't been to El Burrito Jr.'s since the breakup. It's usually crawling with kids from our school who I would rather avoid until the rumors about Brady, Elle, and me die down.

"I don't know, Rosie. I don't really feel like running into anyone."

"It makes it worse when you go into hiding. People will forget about it faster if you can start getting back to your normal life." She nudges my shoulder with her own. "We can sit in the back so we see who comes in before they see us."

I fight the desire to turn her down and stay in my room all night. I know she's right. I know that going out and letting people see that I'm fine will help quiet all the gossip, but it's just so hard to find any motivation to put on makeup or switch out my super-comfy yoga pants for jeans. But Rosie isn't going to give up. "Fine. Just El Burrito Jr.'s," I agree reluctantly.

"Want some help with that?" she teases, pointing to the lopsided bun on my head.

"Nothing crazy."

I can see the relief in her eyes and the hope that I am starting to get back to my old self. "I'll just help you with the flat iron." She stands from the bed and extends a hand, pulling me to my feet, before motioning for me to follow her down the hall to the bathroom we share. There are a few things scattered on the counter, the proof that one teenage girl got ready in here this morning. It wasn't me. I've been doing the bare minimum. It's all I can do to take a shower and brush the tangles out of my hair. I certainly haven't been the one littering the counter with various shades of eye shadow and filling up space with hair products and eyeliners.

Rosie plugs in the flat iron as I rest my hip against the counter. I fold my arms over my chest and watch as she digs around in the drawer until she finds my makeup bag. I wonder if she'll have to blow dust off the top of it. When you're having trouble putting one foot in front of the other, you certainly aren't going to try to creatively enhance your features with colorful goo. The zipper on that poor bag would be rusted soon enough if it didn't get some use.

"Makeover time," she says softly as she blots some foundation on my face. I make duck lips and she laughs. "See, I knew you didn't forget." She goes to work covering the dark bags beneath my eyes and brushing some bronzer over my cheeks and forehead. I close my eyes when she applies the eye shadow and liner.

"Open and look up," she directs as she holds the mascara wand in front of me.

"Poke my eye and I'll hold you down and smear this mess into your hair." I wrap my hand around her wrist and move the wand back closer to her face. Her lips curl up and she blows a kiss.

"Trust me. I do this all the time." Her face gets serious as she braces her hand against my cheek. I do trust her. I trust her to do more than put on my makeup. I trust her to watch out for me and to make sure I will eventually find all my missing pieces that seemed to scatter when Elle and Brady broke me apart. I just can't tell her all of that without the tears that are threatening to spill down my cheeks ruining the work she's done so far to my face.

"There," she says, stepping back to look at the final

result. I look into the mirror and recognize the person I see staring back. She'd somehow managed to paint the image of who I used to be onto the poor, depressed girl that has replaced her.

"Thanks." I smile and give her a hug. She holds on a little tighter and longer than usual, but I don't mind.

"That was the easy part." She reaches for the small black band in my hair and tugs it a few inches. "This is going to hurt." With a few more tugs she pulls it free and tosses it onto the counter by the flat iron. I watch her reflection in the mirror as she concentrates on separating out chunks of my hair and heating them until they hang perfectly straight.

"What if we run into them?" I ask. Her eyes meet mine in the mirror and she gives me a small shrug.

"You know seeing you has to hurt them too." She sets the iron down and runs her fingers through my hair. "Elle must be torn up about what she did." I open my mouth to argue, but Rosie shakes her head. "She's not a monster. She might be a terrible friend, but we both know somewhere in there she has a heart." With Rosie and me being so near in age, she was almost as close to Elle as I was. Elle had even encouraged Rosie to try out for the junior varsity cheer squad, and would help her with the routines—something that the previous varsity cheer captain wouldn't have dreamed of doing.

I nod my head and she reaches for the flat iron again.

"I'm embarrassed," I confess. Rosie pauses for a moment, taking the time to look into my eyes again as I explain. "I feel stupid for not seeing what must have been right under my nose. I feel ashamed that I carried on about how great things were between Brady and me when she was already pulling him away from me."

"You didn't do anything wrong. She's the one who should be embarrassed and ashamed. He's just a boy, Everly. He never should have come between you guys. He showed everyone he's dishonest." We are quiet for a minute as the flat iron slides along my strands again. "He'll never be able to trust her either. He has to know that a person who is capable of doing what she did to you could never be loyal to anyone. His relationship with her is nothing when compared to the length of time and commitment you and Elle had invested in each other. If she could turn her back on you—she can do it to him too."

An hour later as we pull back onto our street after an uneventful dinner, I'm grateful Rosie pushed to get me out of the house. I'm realizing that sometimes when I don't feel like I have the strength to do something on my own, I have people who love me who will pick up the slack and help get me out of this dark hole. Little by little I will dig myself out, but the task is so much easier when people are offering me a hand and cheering me on as I climb back up to the light.

four

MRS. CRAMIER CALLS our student council meeting to order right after the sixth period bell. As the secretary of activities, I'm responsible for keeping a calendar of school events, planning spirit week, and for helping the other council members plan their assigned activities. It's a position I ran for because I'd always enjoyed cheering for the football team but wanted to make sure other athletes and academically strong students were recognized too. (Plus it would be a fun way of supporting Brady and a great excuse to get out of school early to attend the away games.) The end-of-the-year rally is always my favorite event. This year I would get to announce the students who make it into the bigger colleges and honor those who scored high on their SATs.

My job was even more fun than I'd expected because Angie is the secretary of spirit and my right-hand woman. We didn't really know each other at the beginning of the year, but after working together so often during sixth period we've become close. We haven't hung out together outside of student council activities, but we've had hours of time to get to know each other while we plan events we are going to lead, and also while we fill the downtime we have when all our tasks are complete. She helps make student council fun, but even she couldn't distract me from the fact that we would soon have to start organizing prom-related events.

Situation: Prom
Feelings: Embarrassed, angry, hurt, nausea, heartache
Unhelpful Thoughts: I'm going to miss my senior prom
because the boy who promised to take me is taking
my former best friend instead.
Alternative Thoughts: Maybe her dress will be ugly.
Maybe no one will notice I'm not there. Angie can
take pictures for me and it will be just like I was
there.

I don't think this log is helping as much as Laura wants it to. Luckily the topic of this year's prom is only mentioned once by the senior class president when she reminds everyone to start working on the notices that will go up around campus to give students time to save for the price of admission, so I don't have to spend the meeting pretending I'm excited about it.

My hands have finally stopped shaking from my panic attack earlier. I try to focus on the details of our council meeting, but my mind keeps jumping back to the drama of this morning, and how quickly my day spiraled out of control. Everything had been fine when I entered my first period class, but by the end of second period I'd caught wind of a rumor involving me and the boyfriend of my friend Kendall. It was wildly untrue, and I was so grateful Kendall came to talk to me about it instead of just believing what was being said. Feeling like I could do nothing to stop the lies from flying around the school triggered a panic attack, and even though it's been a few hours now I can still feel the surreal out-of-body feeling I experience after suffering a powerful panic attack.

"Everly, will you run this down to Coach Williams?" Mrs. Cramier holds a folded-up sheet of paper in my direction after the conclusion of the meeting, drawing my attention back to the room and out of my dizzying thoughts. I want to tell her no. She has no idea that the thought of an unplanned walk across campus causes anxiety so fierce I fear I might be having a heart attack.

"Sure," I say instead as I scoot my chair back and make my way to the front of the classroom. I tell myself that everyone should be in class. If I can make it back before the bell rings I shouldn't run into either of them.

The halls are clear, but each time I hear a noise coming from a locker bay or hallway I feel as if my heart is trying to leap from my chest. When I open the large doors of the building that houses the pool, the smell of chlorine is so strong it seems to smack me right in the face. I carefully step around the puddles on my way to where Coach Williams is standing at the far end of the large expanse of chemically treated water. For some reason, it feels like it's much warmer in here than other places on campus and I wonder if they try to keep the temperature higher to make the student athletes more comfortable as they climb in and out of the pool.

"Mrs. Cramier asked me to bring you this." I hand him the paper and wait in case it requires his response. Sixth period is usually when the school sports teams practice, and I look around the humid building, noticing the boys filing out of the locker room in their swim gear.

I find myself staring at one guy in particular. It's the boy from the waiting room last week. Gabe. *He goes to my school?*

He's laughing with another kid and I can't help but notice his tan skin and the way his muscles form the ideal swimmer's body—smaller than Brady's, but more toned. Just before covering his eyes with his goggles, he lifts his gaze to me. His smile seems to freeze and then grow wider. He adjusts the goggles and then dives into the pool.

The coach is scribbling something on the paper I handed him so I take a second to watch Gabe swim a length. His strokes are smooth and seamless and it's almost like magic the way he cuts his arms into the water with hardly any splash. It's mesmerizing to watch. "Here, please take this back." The coach hands me the paper and then blows his whistle, calling the boys to attention.

I hurry back to the student council room, trying hard to figure out how I've never seen him here before. I suppose it's because I go to a huge school in a very big city and for the last two and a half years, I've been with Brady, so involved in our relationship that I never really looked around. He might have been here the whole time and I just never noticed. I shake my head as I step inside the noisy room.

I take the note to Mrs. Cramier and then head into the catacomb of rooms in the student activities office to find Angie. When I see her, she is bent over the rally signs we've been working on this week. I sit on the edge of the long paper so she doesn't have to hold it while writing the message down the length of the clean white strip.

"Thanks, Everly." She glances up at me. "It's totally worth the long walk to see the boys in the pool, huh?" She smiles coyly and I feel my cheeks redden. "Oh, come on. I know it hasn't been that long since you and Brady broke up, but prom is coming and it's pretty much an unwritten rule that the secretary of activities has to go. You need to get back out there with your head up and find a date. I could ask Carl to help set you up," she says, swirling the flat marker brush in the shape of an *R*.

"I know. I'll figure it out. Did you get your dress yet?" I hope that she'll be excited enough about the details of her dress that she will forget about my pathetic situation.

"My mom took me last night. I thought she would say no because it's shorter than the one I wore last year, but she said it was still classy so she let me have it." Angie had her eyes on that dress for a month. It was in the window of the most popular dress store at the mall. She'd shown me pictures of it, and I even made a special pass in front of the store the last time Rosie and I went shopping so I could see it in person.

"It's going to look great on you." I move off the paper so we can roll it up and set it aside to work on another one.

"Thanks. Did you buy that red dress you were thinking about?" She stands and rests her hand on her hip. She has been so supportive of me over the whole Brady and Elle situation, I know she's only asking because she cares about how crappy it would be if I had.

"No. I don't think I want to wear that one anymore." I pull the long piece of butcher paper off the roll and she tears off the perfect amount for another sign. We work very well together.

"Probably best to start fresh," she says, squatting down to sit on the end so I can use the markers.

"Tell me about your plans. Are you guys staying close for dinner or driving downtown?"

Angie launches into a description of how she and her boyfriend, Carl, and another couple are going to drive to Santa Monica for dinner so that they can stretch the night out as long as possible. "There's room for two more in the limo," she says, practically singing the words. "You and your date should come with us. It will be good for you to get away from the usual group of people. Come out with us. I can even have Carl set you up with a friend of his from Saint Anthony's."

I give her a noncommittal "maybe." It's sweet of her to offer, but I'm not exactly leaping at the chance to spend the night with a group of people who, with the exception of Angie, I'm not really close to, and a date from the local Catholic school who is probably either going with me because Angie forced him to or because he is hoping that in my vulnerable state I'll hook up with him.

Finally the bell rings, signaling the end of the school day. Angie grabs her backpack as I put away the last few items. "You ready, Angie?" Lisa says from the doorway, giving me a small wave when I look up.

"Yep. I'm ready." She moves toward the exit but turns around right before she steps outside. "You should sit with us at lunch tomorrow. We could talk about prom—or not." She shrugs her shoulders, letting me know she'll help if I need it but won't push.

I pack up my backpack slowly while everyone else files out of the room. The other kids rush to leave, but I know that there is a chance the cheer squad will still be practicing on the front lawn and I want to give them plenty of time to leave the area before I walk to my car.

When I'm sure the coast is clear, I make my way out to the nearly empty parking lot. Out of habit I look for Brady's truck. It's parked in his usual spot in the first row among the other football players' vehicles. Interestingly, I also find myself looking for the big truck from the other day, but it's nowhere in sight.

five

WHEN I GET home I toss my keys onto the small table near the door and head up to my room. I can hear Rosie's music down the hall so I drop my bag off in my room and make my way to her door. I knock a few times. "Come in," she shouts over the song.

"What are you listening to?" I ask, sitting down on the edge of her bed. She's at her desk staring at her homework, but I don't know how she could get anything done with the music on so loud. As if she could read my mind, she reaches up and turns it down.

"It's a new band Dawn told me about. She heard them

on KROQ this morning." She scoots her chair back and stands up so she can join me on her bed. "Today was pretty brutal, huh?"

I shrug my shoulders. "I just feel like this whole thing is getting out of control."

"It's awful," she agrees, lying back on her bed and stuffing a pillow beneath her head. "People said they saw you and Kendall talking after third period."

"She was waiting for me outside my class. Honestly, she'll never know how much I appreciate her asking me about what was being said instead of just believing it."

"It's crazy. By the time I got to cheer I'd been asked by four different people if you and Kendall were really going to fight."

I shake my head and let out a breath. "Kendall knew the stories were out of hand, but she wanted to find out if I knew where they started." I move up next to Rosie and rest my head on her pillow. She's now picking at her nail polish.

"Did you tell her Elle started it?"

"We don't know that for sure," I say, turning my head so I can see her face better.

"She might not have said what was going around by the end of the day, but I know for a fact she told Heather that you told her you liked Kendall's boyfriend. Heather told me she's the one who told Kendall." Rosie pulls a large piece of her polish off.

"The only thing I can remember is saying he's cute after seeing a prom picture of Kendall with her date last year. How Elle twisted that into liking him, I have no idea." I cross my legs and kick my foot up and down. Rosie mimics my position.

"I don't even know her anymore," she says with disgust. "She's really making a mess of things."

"I don't understand why she's stirring up so much drama. She already has Brady, why does she feel the need to go around and light a bunch of fires to my other friendships?" I pause, glancing over at Rosie. "The thing is, I did say some things about our friends—not anything terrible," I say quickly, "but I definitely vented to her."

Rosie looks at me again. "We all say things. We all have opinions. You never meant for any of that to actually be heard by the person. She's not playing fair. I think she might just be panicking. Maybe she's trying to get people on her side before they have a chance to think about what it says about her that she's capable of doing what she did to her best friend. With all the facts, people will think she's terrible."

"Because she is terrible," I say softly, but it still hurts to say something bad about her. I wonder when I'll get over that. I have all the facts and there is still a part of me that doesn't want to believe it's true.

"It just seems like she's changed so much," Rosie says, and I realize that deep down she is struggling with it too.

"I think that's the part that hurts the most. If she were acting like the same old Elle, I'd eventually get over what she did with Brady. But every day it seems like there's something else she's done to unravel our friendship."

"What are you going to do about it?" Rosie flips over onto her stomach so she can see me better.

"What can I do? There's no way of knowing what she's going to say or do next."

"Why don't you talk to her? Maybe then she'll stop starting rumors out of desperation." I think about it for a minute.

"The thing is, I was willing to hear her out when she called me that night after I found out about her and Brady. But the fact that she said she was sorry, and then followed it up with 'but,' like there was anything that could follow that word that would justify what they'd done, just hurt way too much. That's why I hung up and haven't been accepting her calls. Besides, she may have said 'sorry' but her actions are showing me a different story. Hooking up with Brady might have been a mistake, but everything she did after that showed me her character. She's not the kind of person I want in my life."

Rosie nods her head. "I get it. And if Brady and Elle are

out of your life, then they're out of mine too. I just wish getting them out of your life fixed it, you know? I want you to start feeling better."

"I want to feel better too. I want to go to sleep and wake up months from now when all the rumors have passed and no one can even remember a time when Elle and I were friends. I just want to completely fall off the social radar. If I knew how to fast-forward my life to a time when walking on campus didn't give me a panic attack I'd do it."

"There might not be anything we can do to erase them from your life, but maybe you could do something for yourself that would show people you don't care anymore."

"Any ideas?" I tease, kicking her foot with my own.

"Actually, I've been thinking. Do you remember last year when Dawn's boyfriend broke up with her? She started dating again right away. I thought it was strange that she was talking to other boys when she still seemed brokenhearted, but she told me it helped, even though she knew that it probably wouldn't work out with any of the guys. I don't know . . . maybe it would help you to get back out there." Her voice sounds so hopeful.

"I'm not ready for that," I say adamantly. "I just don't think I could talk to another guy yet. What if I always compare him to Brady? What if he hurts me worse than Brady did?" I chew nervously on my lip.

"Not all guys are like that. What about someone from student council? Or maybe have a friend set you up with a boy who doesn't even go to our school." Her face lights up with the idea.

"I'll think about it." I don't have the heart to tell her that I don't think I'll be ready to trust someone for a long time.

I hear the front door open and the clanking sound of Mom's keys as she tosses them onto the table. "Girls? I'm home."

"We're up here," we say in unison and then giggle. My mom makes her way up the stairs and then opens the bedroom door.

"Dad is stuck in a meeting. I'm too tired to cook and I've really been craving that Italian restaurant with the fresh-baked bread. What do you say we go out tonight and you can tell me all about your day?" She leans against the doorway and I can see how tired she is. Yet even with everything she has on her plate, she's been there for me through all of this. I smile at her and then at my sister, feeling truly grateful to have such an amazing support group.

"I'm in!" Rosie shouts, jumping up from the bed and then offering me a hand to help me up. I'm not very hungry, and the stress of the day has made my stomach hurt, but I won't miss the chance to spend time with my mom and Rosie.

"All right. I'm in too." Rosie pulls me up to my feet and

the relief on their faces does not go unnoticed by me. It makes me want to work harder on getting myself back together. As Rosie slips on her shoes, my mom pulls me into a tight hug, resting her cheek on my head.

"I'm proud of you, kiddo. Baby steps."

six

A FEW DAYS later as I'm driving to Laura's office, I find myself wondering if I will see Gabe again. I haven't thought about him much since I saw him at swim practice, but I'm still curious what his story is. I'm a little surprised at the quick pang of disappointment I feel when I see that the waiting room is empty. I take my usual spot on the couch and flip open the book to my place.

A few minutes later the door beside the couch swings open and I look up for just a second to watch him slip in. I haven't been in here for longer than five minutes, which means we have another five or so before our appointment times. There are only two other people in here now, scattered around the room and reading magazines. I hold my breath, wondering if he'll sit down beside me again, but pretending to read and trying not to be obvious.

I watch his feet as they pass in front of me, just barely visible over the top of my page. The couch cushion dips with his weight as he settles in on the other edge.

I debate with myself whether I should say anything to him, acknowledge that I saw him at school, for another minute before my curiosity about who he is gets the best of me. "You smell like chlorine," I whisper, glancing over at him, my lips curling up in a smile.

"I live in that damn pool," he says, pulling his hoodie up to his nose to investigate.

"Do you play on the water polo team?" I take my eyes from the page and look into his. Another color I hadn't noticed before. I'd seen the blue and green last time, but now there are little flecks of yellow that seem to glow when he smiles.

"Yep. It's my fourth year on the team. I've played on private teams since second grade. Today was just swim practice, though."

"Wow, that's a long time to stick with a sport. Why water polo?"

"My dad played water polo in high school and college.

He was even in the Junior Olympics. He thought it could be something we could practice together. He's pretty busy now with work, but he never misses a game."

"That's so great he did that. I'm a little embarrassed to say I've never been to a game. I'm the secretary of activities and just recently I realized I attend less than a quarter of the activities at our school. Kind of stupid, really."

"You should come. It's pretty intense."

"I'll be sure to. Why haven't I ever seen you around campus?" I ask him quietly. The lady across from us is looking over her magazine to sneak a peek in our direction. I smile at her and she smiles back before lifting the glossy mag up again.

"You probably have seen me, actually. We had Spanish together our freshman year." I feel my brows pull together. Surely I would have noticed him. When I don't say anything he chuckles. "I looked a lot different. I've grown an entire foot since then. I sat in the back."

"You'll have to excuse me. I'm finding that I've apparently had my head up my ass for a few years." He laughs and the woman is back to watching us, clearly more entertained by our conversation than by what she is reading.

"Don't worry about it. It's not important. It makes sense, though." He rubs his hand along the very short hair on his head.

"What makes sense?" I ask him, looking hard at the inquisitive woman until she goes back to her reading.

"You having your head up your ass. It explains the whole Brady Taylor phase. It makes a little more sense now." When I look back at him he winks.

"Is that what that was?" I ask, smiling. It's oddly reassuring to hear someone teasing me about liking Brady instead of feeling sorry for me for having lost him to Elle. Although I won't deny that a little part of my heart protests with an ache, as if trying to remind me that it once would have bothered me to hear someone say anything negative about Brady.

"Clearly." For the first time since the breakup, I laugh. Not a forced laugh to appease my mom or sister, but a genuine laugh that even has the woman behind the desk shooting looks in our direction.

His therapist opens his office door first. He stands up, but instead of going in he turns to me. "I hope this doesn't seem weird, but I've read everything John Green has written, and I noticed last time you were carrying around his latest." He pulls a book out of his hoodie pocket and says, "Have you read this one yet?"

"No, but I was actually thinking about picking it up this weekend. I've only read one of his books and now I can't wait to get my hands on all of them."

His cheeks lift slightly in a smile as he holds it out for me to take. "You should read this next. It's my favorite of his."

I nod my head and take it from his hand. "Thank you."

He ducks his head, tucks his spiral notebook under his arm, and then walks into the office. I flip open the book and see that *Gabe* is written in black ink along with a phone number. I'm not really sure how but even though he is practically a stranger it feels like Gabe is already a friend. I'm smiling when Laura opens her door and asks me if there's anything new.

seven

THE NEXT DAY I grab my lunch bag from my locker and keep my head down as I make my way over to where I've been eating lunch for the last few weeks. While I was never as close to anyone else in our group as I was with Brady and Elle, I genuinely considered them my friends. I thought they felt the same way, but now that Brady and I are over, I feel like I lost some of them in the split. Sure, my old friends talk to me in class or when he isn't around, but the way things happened between the three of us makes navigating a group setting a little awkward.

If I wanted to sit where I used to sit while I was with

Brady, I imagine no one would tell me to leave, but having the three of us in the same place at the same time might interrupt the casual flow of conversation. I hate to make situations awkward and I don't want our friends to feel like they're in the middle, even though I'm still hurt that some of them knew about the betrayal and chose not to tell me. Also, I'm just not ready to spend my lunch hour watching Brady and Elle hang all over each other or listening to them talking about their plans for the weekend. I know I shouldn't be avoiding it, but it feels so much safer to eat somewhere else.

My snack break and lunch are now spent keeping my head down and finding open classrooms or less crowded quads to hang out in. I work on homework or read so that my eyes aren't constantly darting around. At first, a few of the groups that weren't used to me sitting near them seemed disturbed. They lowered their voices or tightened their circles, but when they saw that I was content to sit alone and not try to awkwardly join them, they went back to business as usual.

I set my backpack onto the old wooden bench that circles one of the large trees growing in the quad. Sitting down next to it, I pull out Gabe's book and reach for my lunch before spinning my body around so I can lie back against my bag. I lift my feet up onto the bench and then open the book above my face so it blocks out the bright afternoon sun. It's pretty weather for May in California, with the sun shining down and just a hint of a breeze to keep you comfortable. I stayed up really late last night reading the book because I fell in love with the story, but there should be enough left to get me through the next thirty-five minutes.

"Why do you insist on sitting here alone?" My sister's voice pulls me from the story. "You should still sit with your group. Just because you and Brady aren't together anymore doesn't mean those people aren't still your friends."

I let the book fall to my chest and block the shining sun with a hand over my brow. "Hello, Rosie. Sometimes I just like to be alone." I let my eyes drift over to her friend Dawn, standing next to her. She gives me a wave.

Rosie rolls her eyes and leans closer to whisper, "You're letting them win. Why aren't you fighting back?"

I study her pained face for a minute. "Some battles you just can't win. The best you can do is hope to be alive when it's over. I think I just need to survive this."

"You're so dramatic," she says with a sigh. "That doesn't make any sense. I know you and Elle will never be friends again, but if you keep avoiding that area, you are going to lose your other friendships too."

"I think you're missing the part where it's completely awkward whenever the three of us are in the same general area. No one wants to be a part of that tension . . . and that's not even taking into account how everyone feels about the rumors Elle's been spreading." I wave my hand, brushing away the imaginary tension in the picture I'd just painted for her.

"Whatever. I think you should start telling people what really happened. Ruin Elle's reputation like she's trying to do to you. Don't just sit over here all alone and let people think you aren't important. Make the friends who knew and didn't tell you look you in the eye. If you want to sit with us you can, but I think you should march right over to your old table and eat your lunch with your friends." Rosie glances around the courtyard, trying to assess the damage I have already done to my popularity by being here alone. I move my foot from the bench and give her a little kick.

"I'll be fine. Go eat lunch with your friends." I lift my foot again and nudge her playfully. I can tell by her expression she doesn't want to leave me alone, but she nods her head and links her arm through Dawn's.

"We aren't practicing on the front lawn today. Coast will be clear after sixth period." She slaps away my foot. "I'll meet you outside of student council to get a ride home."

"You don't have practice after school at all?" I ask.

"Not today. Coach has an appointment. We're practicing inside the gym and then we're free to go when the bell rings."

"All right. Dawn, if you need a ride, meet up with us. If Rosie isn't bugging you that is." Rosie rolls her eyes again at my words, but both of them are laughing.

"Thanks, Everly," Dawn answers over her shoulder as my sister pulls her away from me and back in the direction of the main lunch tables.

eight

ROSIE REACHES FOR the radio but I slap her hand away before she can change the station. "Don't touch," I warn as she gives me a pouty face.

"Come on, Everly. I can't even hear myself think over this crap."

"That's the point," I practically shout over the beating music, but turn the volume down because she isn't exaggerating. I slide my sunglasses on as I wait for the slow line of cars to leave the student parking lot.

"How long did it take you to start feeling better after you and Jay broke up last year?" Rosie turns in her seat and asks Dawn. I move my gaze up to the rearview mirror so I can see her face as she sits in the back seat of my car.

"Hmm." She purses her lips and squints her eyes as she thinks of the answer. "Maybe a couple months." Her eyes meet mine in the mirror. "I'm not sure the exact amount of time. It just sort of happened one day."

"What do you mean?" I ask as I finally get a chance to pull out of the parking lot and onto the two-lane street in front of the school.

"Well, I was pretty sick about it for the first month. My sister told me I should start going out with other guys. She said sometimes it's easier to get over an old boyfriend if you have a new one. At first I didn't believe her, but after a few weeks of feeling totally miserable, I was willing to try anything, so I let her set me up with one of her friends who was a senior at West. We only went out on a couple of dates, but I think just doing that helped me not think about Jay so much. I think dating made me realize my world didn't have to revolve around Jay, so I started feeling better."

"See," Rosie grumbles, nudging me in the side with her elbow.

"You're about to lose shotgun. Abuse the privilege and I'll let Dawn take your spot." We all laugh when Rosie blows me a raspberry.

"I think you should try it." Rosie's words are a mix of hope and pleading.

"I think *you* should try dating," I counter. Rosie's never had a boyfriend. She has a lot of guy friends who she's constantly texting, but I think she has a bad habit of putting them in the friend zone without giving them a chance to be anything more.

Rosie rolls down her window, sticking her entire arm out to wave at a group of kids crossing the street. "I'd love to try dating, but that would require a guy to actually seem interested in me."

"Reese told me he thought you were cute," Dawn chimes in from the back seat, her hair blowing around her face until she gives Rosie's seat a good shove. "Close the window, social butterfly."

"Reese is taking Mindy to prom. If he thought I was cute, he would have asked me."

"If he was that into Mindy, he wouldn't have brought you up during science lab and asked me a million questions about you." Dawn finally gets control of her hair as Rosie finishes putting up the window. She doesn't respond to Dawn, but I can see that she likes what she heard. She's surprisingly shy when it comes to having crushes. It's the only area of her social life she seems to struggle with.

I pull into Dawn's driveway and wait until I'm sure she gets into her house before I drive away. With just Rosie and me in the car, I reach to turn the music back up. Rosie stops my hand with her own before I can move the dial. "I have something I want to tell you about." My stomach instantly sinks with her words. I feel the rush of heat spread through my body and that quick flutter of my heart that usually serves as a warning that a panic attack is coming on.

"What is it?"

"I heard today that Brady is going to ask Elle to prom." She watches my face for a minute, waiting for me to say something. Or maybe she's waiting for me to fall apart. When I say nothing, she continues, "I just wanted to give you a chance to get used to the idea before it happens. I'm sorry. I know you really wanted to go with him. It sucks that this all blew up before you got to check that off the list."

I'd been looking forward to going to prom with Brady since we started planning it in student council months ago. Every time we discussed a new detail, I imagined being there with him. When we chose the theme song I pictured dancing to it in his arms. When we chose the location, I had voted for the aircraft museum because I could picture wandering around beneath the old planes with him when we got bored with dancing. I was planning the perfect evening for us, so it really hurt to see Elle and Brady in my imagination instead.

Her hand moves out to squeeze my shoulder. I draw in a big breath and then let it go slowly. I focus my attention on the small white lines that seem to speed beneath our car. I do everything I can to fight off the panic attack that tries to take flight in my chest. *This is not a threat. I'm okay.* I repeat the words over and over until I start feeling myself regain control over my fiercely beating heart. "Thank you," I manage between breaths.

"It's going to be fine. You'll feel better by then," Rosie reassures me.

I stare out the front windshield as we wait at the light. I hate Elle. I hate Brady. I hate prom. But most of all, I hate that seeing me hurt seems to steal the joy out of Rosie. "Boys are awful," she says. When the light finally changes, she reaches down to the stereo and cranks the volume up until I can practically feel the vibration of the sound waves against my eardrums. I wonder if she's thinking about Reese not asking her to prom, because if so, I'm kind of hating him too.

We might not be able to agree on our choice of music or the decibel level at which it should be played, but in this moment we both can agree that prom and boys inflict unnecessary pain on a teenage girl's heart. And sometimes screaming out the angry lyrics of a heavy metal song is the only thing that can be done to stop from falling apart. So we sing until our voices are hoarse and the palms of our hands tingle from pounding out the rhythm on the dash and steering wheel. It doesn't fix everything, but for the two minutes it takes us to drive the last block home, we are too busy laughing and singing to notice any hurt in our hearts.

nine

I STRUGGLED WITH anxiety Wednesday night and all day Thursday after Rosie told me what she'd heard about Brady asking Elle to prom. By Friday morning I've used every tool Laura has taught me to get my thoughts away from them and onto something else. That something else turned out to be Gabe. I've been thinking about texting him since the moment I saw his phone number inside the cover of the book. It's been a few days since he gave it to me. I've even typed out a message three times and erased it. He just seems like someone who could be a friend. I realize that we only talked for a couple minutes, but he seemed silly and playful, and I get the feeling he's smart too. I try not to think too much about the fact that I also find him cute, though it's hard not to after the conversation that Rosie and I had. I don't have any intention of getting into a relationship with him, but maybe an additional perk of getting to know Gabe better is that his attractiveness would help distract me from thinking about Brady.

Would it be weird to text him? I wonder for the millionth time, staring down at my phone. Maybe I should just wait until I see him again at our appointments on Tuesday. My fingers pause for a moment above the shining letters before once again typing out the message.

ME: Hi Gabe, it's Everly Morgan. I finished the book.

I hit send and then wait as the message is marked delivered. My heart rate picks up and I tell myself it's okay if he doesn't respond.

As I continue to look at the phone, willing a message from him to pop up, the event notification on my phone calendar dings with a reminder that prom is four weeks away. I pull the thought log out and flatten it against my desk. I want to make sure to share the news about prom with Laura.

Situation: Brady asking Elle to prom
Feelings: Disappointed, unfixable, anxious, hurt
Unhelpful Thoughts: This is my worst nightmare coming

true. This is really the end of us. Prom pictures are
permanent.

Alternative Thoughts: I can hide in my room and pretend
it isn't happening and no one will notice. (Just
kidding, Laura.) Prom is not the most important
event that will happen in my life.

I fold the paper back up and slip it into the cover of
the book I picked up at the library. I usually get books that
revolve around relationships, but this time I decided to
expand my horizons and go for something dystopian. Fine, I
might also have liked the idea of teenage death matches. Just
when I'm about to swing my backpack over my shoulder to
head to school, my phone chimes with a text.

GABE: What did you think?

ME: You were right. It's amazing.

GABE: Totally.

ME: Thanks for letting me borrow it. I'll bring it Tuesday
if you'll be there.

GABE: I'll be there.

I have so much I want to talk to my therapist about on
Tuesday, and now that I know Gabe will be in the waiting
room, I'm eager to get through the next few days, which I
already know are going to feel especially long thanks to all
the work I have to get started on for student council. Prom

is approaching and that means I'll be busy with helping to design the posters and flyers to promote the dance. I already helped scope out the sites earlier this year and gave my input on any vendors we were going to hire to make it a success. I can't believe how quickly the time has flown by and that soon everyone is going to begin pairing up so they can buy their tickets.

My mother told me that when she was in high school, asking someone to prom was not a big deal. Couples would automatically go together without any big production, and singles asked out other singles over lunch or in between classes. I wish my generation were more like hers. We have made some advances, such as allowing same-sex couples to go together, but we have turned the invite into a social production on the grandest scale. To make matters worse, the school staff has joined in on the craziness, and a limo ride to the dance will be given to the couple with the most unique and epic invite. All students who participate will have their names on a ballot, and our entire student body will vote in their homerooms the day before our big prom rally.

Prom is four weeks away, whether I'm ready to face that night or not. The tickets go on sale today at lunch, and I was excused from my first period class to help hang the posters advertising our theme and ticket prices. "Stay with Me" sounded great as a theme when I voted on it at the beginning of the year. I had pictured Brady and me dancing in our formal wear beneath the lights of a disco ball, my head on his chest as we talked about going away to college together. Now I imagine myself watching him dance with Elle as I silently beg him to stay with me.

I've been on edge all morning, scampering from class to class in an attempt to avoid any over-the-top invites that might be happening in the hallways. By third period, the school is abuzz with stories of prom invites. I hear that someone released at least a hundred balloons to get the attention of his prospective prom date on the third floor of building three. Another guy set up his electric guitar on the steps of the auditorium so he could play his girlfriend "their song."

At least I don't have to worry about seeing Brady ask Elle. We talked about it when we were together, and he told me it wasn't his thing to embarrass himself in front of everyone, that he'd just ask me some private way so that it would be more intimate—something only he and I knew the details of. At least that's the *Alternative Thought* I keep repeating to myself so that I won't break down in a puddle of tears every time I see a poster or hear a story of how someone has been asked.

My grandma used to tell me that I shouldn't put negative energy out there. She believed you could make something bad happen just by thinking about it. I never believed her, but as I leave my third period class, I step into a quad decorated with brown and gold streamers, our school colors, twisting in the breeze above us. I'm on the ground level of a two-story building when what seems like the entire football team and cheer squad fill the second floor railing.

Our school song starts playing from the speakers of a very old boom box, being lifted above everyone's heads. As I watch, the boom box appears to float toward me through the crowd and I feel my heart struggle to pump through the fear and pain that are choking it. I know the hands that are gripping that boom box. I know them because for years I held them—traced each crease with my fingers as we shared secrets.

Brady's eyes meet mine and his brilliant smile falters. He quickly looks away and I know the moment when he finds Elle's eyes because his cheeks lift again with happiness. She saunters into the quad and throws her hands up to her mouth perfectly, just as if some great Hollywood screenwriter has scripted it. Brady sets down the boom box and lowers himself to one knee as the entire female population lets out a collective sigh.

I pull my eyes away from the scene in front of me and feel my legs begin to weaken beneath me. I turn and take off running, not caring that the whole student body can see me. It's far less embarrassing then being seen sobbing hysterically.

The girls' bathroom door is within reach as I push my way past the last few students on their way to the big show. A strong hand grips my elbow and pulls me backward, tugging me into the boys' bathroom instead. My thoughts are scattered and I start to protest, but Gabe spins me around and holds me by my elbows.

"It's better in here," he assures me gently. "No girls."

I nod, but a sob breaks free and I pull my elbows from him so I can cover my face. He hesitates for a moment and then his warm arms encircle me, pulling me to his chest, rubbing the back of my head as I proceed to unravel. I hear the door begin to squeak open, but Gabe growls, "Get the fuck out," and it closes again quickly. He lets me go and grabs the rim of the large metal trash can sitting outside the stalls and drags it over to the door, barricading us inside safely. Then his arms are around me again.

My face is pressed into his chest and I feel the slow beat of his heart against my skin. Deep breath in and slowly out. Repeat. I finally stop whimpering and instead fight the small hiccups that have taken over. He doesn't let go of me, keeping me pressed into him, slowly rocking as I try to pull myself together.

His voice is barely a whisper, yet deep and rough. "That was the worst eighties remake I've ever seen. He's an idiot and she deserves him. Does he even realize that our school colors are hideous? Brown and gold. Show me one romantic thing that comes in brown and gold. Pink, maybe. Red. I'm not an expert, but I think he fucked that up."

A small laugh escapes my lips, and while I know he's just trying to make me feel better, I don't fight it because it's kind of working. "Yellow. I've seen yellow." I feel him smile against my head.

"Yes, yellow can be romantic. Not brown."

"Thank you," I whisper as I pull away. His head tips to the side as he takes in my puffy wet face. A small frown turns his lips just before he pulls the sleeve of his hoodie down over his hand and raises it up to dry the tears from my cheek. As I watch him through my tear-filled eyes, I wonder why he's being so nice to me. We barely know each other.

As if reading my mind he says, "Sorry if that was weird that I grabbed you like that. You seemed upset when you ran past and I figured you'd want some privacy." I smile weakly at him and lift my shirt at the collar and wipe my own face. I quickly realize my mistake when I see that my white shirt is streaked with black mascara and is see-through in a few spots. Of course today would be the first day I tried to put on a little makeup again.

When I look back up, Gabe is smiling at me but trying to hide it in case I don't find it funny. "Here," he says as he lowers his backpack to the ground and reaches for the bottom of his hoodie. When he begins to lift it over his head, the shirt underneath moves slightly with it and I catch a glimpse of the hard, tan plane of his abs above the waistband of his low-slung jeans. "Take this." He hands me the warm, dark hoodie so that I can cover my shirt. I let my backpack slip from my shoulders and then pull the soft fabric over my head, breathing in his scent as it moves over my face.

"Thanks." I step over to the sinks and take in my image in the mirror. I look terrible. "And thank you for pulling me in here. You must think I'm crazy."

"Right, because watching your ex-boyfriend ask your best friend to prom should be a real joy."

"You always this nice to girls who cry at school?" I turn around and lean against one of the sinks.

"I don't know. I've never seen any other girl who was alone while it happened." He shrugs his shoulders. "Usually that's something covered by girl code."

"Girl code?" I cross my arms over my chest.

"Yes. Girl cries, friends immediately swarm and offer reassuring affirmations that seem to pull her through." He takes a step closer and lifts a finger, slowly rotating it as if to show my general area. His eyes move from mine long enough to take a quick look around. "You're missing your swarm."

I nod my head in agreement. "My swarm was a little busy watching my nightmare play out in the quad." He laughs softly and nods his head as well. He moves beside me and turns so he can sit on the edge of the sink. When I see that it doesn't fall from the wall, I pull myself up too. It's interesting that taking my weight off my feet also makes my shoulders feel lighter. It probably has more to do with having a friend to share this moment with than gravity.

"Well, then, it's a good thing I was there." He nudges my shoulder with his own.

"What class am I making you late for?"

"AP English."

"How is it? I love English, but I didn't want to take on too much. I'm in AP chemistry and AP history." Hearing he has an AP class makes me happy that we might have more than our therapists' waiting room in common.

"It's cool. I've always loved reading, but I hated that in all my English classes the teachers seemed to be bogged down by trying to get the kids who didn't read the book to participate. In AP, everyone can follow along with the topic and has something to add to the discussion. It's my only AP class. We can't all handle two AP classes." His shoulder nudges mine again as he teases me. I push back against it.

"Maybe I can't handle it," I say with a sigh. "I thought taking AP classes would make it easier to get into a good college, and I'd be able to skip some of the intro level classes next year, but I hadn't really planned on having to overcome some serious high school drama right when I'm supposed to be studying for the exams."

"It'll be worth it in the end. High school drama stays in high school."

"I hope so. I used to think this would be the best part of being here. I was so sure that the end of my senior year was going to be epic. I'd have great grades, go to parties, hang out with my friends, and spend time with my boyfriend. I actually had a little anxiety thinking about how sad I was going to be when prom was over and I'd graduated." I look into his empathetic eyes. "Now I have anxiety that it won't be over soon enough." The school bell rings loud out in the hallway and echoes off the walls around us.

"I think everyone should be in class now if you want to make an escape." He slides off the sink and onto his feet. "I'll walk you."

I'm already shaking my head. "I'm not going back to class. I don't want anyone to see me like this." I wipe my face one more time, clearing away the last of the tears that had fallen on my cheeks.

"I can get you out the back gate if you want to go home."

"Really? That would be amazing. I don't want you to get in trouble, though." I slide off the sink and stand facing him.

"I won't get in trouble, but it'll go down as a truancy for you."

"I don't care. I can't go to class like this. Everyone will know they made me cry." I turn around to splash some cold water on my face and then use rough brown paper towels to dry it. We put on our backpacks and I consider giving him back his book now, but there is something about knowing I have a reason to sit by him on Tuesday that makes me decide against it.

He was right, everyone has gone to class by the time we move the trash can, push open the door, and step out into the empty hallway. He stops for a second and pulls the hood up over my head and then grabs my hand. I hadn't noticed until now that I've missed holding hands. I let him pull me toward the back gate as we both scan the quad for teachers. Our school's pool is open to the public on the weekends when there isn't a swim meet or polo game, so there is a gate that makes it possible for people to come on campus without going through the main entrance.

When we reach the combination padlock on the visitors' gate, he lets go of my hand and picks up the lock. His fingers move quickly, spinning the dial back and forth until the lock clicks open and he can push the gate far enough for me to slip through. Once I'm on the other side he returns the lock and spins the dial. His hands reach up and hang on to the chain link in front of him.

"I'll see you Tuesday for our appointments?" His tone

makes it sound more like a question than a statement. I'm looking forward to seeing him again.

"I'll be there."

He smiles and nods his head. I turn around and head for my car, telling myself the sooner I get there, the sooner I can pull the loose fabric of his sweatshirt up to my face again and let his scent wipe away the bad events of today.

ten

BOTH OF MY parents work Monday through Friday, which means when I come home during school hours I get the place completely to myself. I toe my shoes off once I'm in my room and drop my backpack to the floor. I should be doing homework since skipping my classes today will mean even more work for me next week, but I need to escape, so I pull my paperback out and throw myself onto my bed.

I try to concentrate on the words on the page, but when I get to the end of a paragraph I have no idea what I've just read. After a few minutes I give up and toss the book down on the floor beside my bed. It's times like these that I think about calling Elle. I know she would answer because she's been trying to talk to me since that dreadful morning I discovered her with Brady, but I won't give her a chance. And that's why I can't call her, I remind myself. I wouldn't be speaking to my friend, I'd be talking to someone who has repeatedly hurt me, who has used the things I told her in the strictest confidence to separate me from the people I thought were my friends, even as she tried to apologize to me. My best option is to stick to my plan of keeping my distance from her, because a conversation with her could only lead to an epic verbal bashing or the agreement that we would never be friends again. I'm not emotionally strong enough to handle either of those options. I remind myself for the thousandth time that missing someone doesn't mean they were right for you—it just means it's hard to watch them go.

I had worried so much about Brady asking Elle to prom, but the worst part about today wasn't so much that he asked her, but how he asked her. The Brady I knew would never have made a big show of asking me to prom. In fact one time last summer when Brady and I were hanging out we pulled out an old yearbook and flipped through the pages. Both of us lay on our stomachs on my bed and laughed at all the pictures of the over-the-top invites. It's completely uncharacteristic of him to put on such a show after being so sure that he would not willingly subject himself to that sort of humiliation even if he knew for sure the girl would accept.

Whether the over-the-top prom invite was something he thought was a great idea, or Elle convinced him he should do it, I don't know. But I feel a heavy ball of dread sink low in my stomach as I think about all the ways he's changed from the person who he used to be. And a small part of me can't help but wonder if the reason he always said he wouldn't ask me to prom in some elaborate way was because he just didn't care enough about me.

My phone vibrates inside my bag, and I drag myself to the edge of my bed and fish it out of the pouch. Brady's name slides across the top of the screen and I wonder if it's possible he could sense that I was thinking about him. I feel my heart race and my hands grow shaky. He hasn't texted me since the morning I found out about Elle.

BRADY: I'm sorry about today. I forgot you were in Elle's building third period.

My pounding heart takes a minute to stumble on its own rhythm before sputtering to a painful achy throb. Laura would want me to focus on the apology, but my brain keeps screaming that it's not *her* building. I've just decided that it isn't worth responding when he sends another text.

BRADY: Whatever. I just needed you to know I didn't do it on purpose, for what it's worth.

ME: Which part wasn't on purpose? The part where you asked the girl you were seeing behind my back to a dance you know I have to attend, or the part where you did it in such a way that every one of our friends watched you choose her over me again? I'm just trying to follow along.

BRADY: Maybe one day you'll forgive me and stop seeing everything I do as an attack on you.

ME: And maybe someday you will think about me and what it might be like to have to watch you move on so quickly. She was my best friend. I can't even run to her to help me through losing you.

BRADY: We didn't do it to hurt you. It just happened. She can still be your friend and I can be a friend too.

ME: Thanks, but I think I'll be choosing my friends a little more wisely in the future.

I know he won't respond, but I stare at my phone for ten minutes before I let the screen go dark. I reach for the zipper of my bag and grab a pen from the smallest front pouch. The paperback beside my bed is still within my reach and I flip through the pages until the worn piece of notebook paper springs free.

Situation: Brady is sorry I screwed up his epic invitation by being a part of their perfect world.

Feelings: Angry, hurt, alone. Heartache of epic
proportions.
Unhelpful Thoughts: I'm an intruder on the perfect life
he is creating without me.
Alternative Thoughts: Maybe this breakup gives him
uncomfortable feelings too. Not the same as mine, but
equally heavy.

I fold the paper up, tuck it back into my book, and then roll onto my back. I pull the hood of Gabe's sweatshirt around my head, drawing the strings tight so that only my nose sticks out of the dark fabric. I think about calling my mom, but I know it will only make her worry about me, so I just sit in the silence.

I think about the retirement home and all the residents that I miss talking to. I feel guilty for canceling my shifts. Then I think about my running shoes in my open closet. I loosen the hood and help it off. I turn my head and look at them, one on its side like I left them weeks ago. I consider going for a run, but can't seem to muster up any excitement for the idea. Instead I continue to lie on my bed, replaying the prom proposal over and over in my head.

The rest of the morning passes quietly. Around lunchtime I think for a minute about making a sandwich, but nothing sounds good. It's not until two o'clock that I finally come out of the warm cocoon of Gabe's hoodie. Rosie texts me to ask if I'm okay and to see where I'm hiding. I tell her I'm fine and that I left school and came home. I know she's going to call Mom and tell her because it might appear that this is becoming routine. She's probably freaking out.

When my phone rings a few minutes later I already know who it is. "Hi, Mom."

"Your sister is worried about you. She said you left school today. This can't become a habit. What's going on?" My mom doesn't sound angry, just concerned. Maybe she's worried I'll never get past this.

"He asked her to prom today."

"Oh, Everly, I'm so sorry. That had to sting." I feel the knot in my throat grow with her words. "Do you need me to come home? I might be able to move a few appointments around."

"You don't have to. I'll be okay. I see Laura on Tuesday." I want my mom to be here with me, but I know it won't be enough. She's hugged me at least fifty times since Brady broke my heart, but her arms don't fill the empty space in my chest and I know that my inability to get myself together shouldn't affect the lives of her patients.

"Okay, sweetheart. I'll be home early tonight. We can watch a show after dinner if you're up to it. Maybe a comedy?"

"Thanks, Mom. I love you." I don't tell her I know I won't be up to it. I'll want to climb into bed, longing for the few hours my brain can shut down.

"I love you more."

By the time Rosie gets home from school I've managed to clean myself up a bit. I don't put on makeup after I wash my face, but I do brush my hair and smooth some country apple lotion on my neck and chest. I've taken off Gabe's hoodie and folded it so that I can return it Tuesday at our appointments. Rosie peeks into my room and smiles when she sees I'm not a complete disaster.

"It was lame. I think Shane is going to outdo him when he asks Lizzy." She pushes open my door and sits next to Gabe's hoodie on my bed. I watch as she runs her fingers across the black fabric. "Who does this belong to?"

"A friend." I unzip my backpack, trying to act nonchalant about her question.

"Like, a guy friend?" She smiles at me and I can see the curiosity in her eyes. I tilt my head and raise my brows.

"He's just a friend, Rosie. Don't go getting all excited." I pick up the sweatshirt and hold it to my chest, not wanting her to touch it anymore.

"Heather said she saw you with some boy during third period. I thought she was crazy." Her legs are crossed and she's now leaning back on her hands, kicking her foot up and down at an excited pace.

"Maybe Heather should worry more about herself than other people. It's like she's allergic to minding her own business." I motion for Rosie to get out of my room. She laughs and jumps to her feet.

"Fine, but I want all the details about this 'friend' so I don't have to hear them from the girls at practice." She leaves my room and I follow her. I lean against the doorframe as I watch her walking down the hall.

"I don't understand why anyone is talking about me at your practice."

"Everly, you have no idea how much those girls envy you. You're smart and pretty. Once you stop trying to hide from everyone, boys are going to be lining up for a chance to go out with you."

"Promise me something then," I say as I look into her eyes.

"Anything."

"Slap me if I ever think about handing my heart over to a boy again." I mean it. I need her to be a part of my recovery plan. She can stand guard over my heart, since I clearly have been careless with it. She rolls her eyes at my declaration as she steps into her room and shuts the door.

eleven

AFTER MY EXCHANGE with Rosie I spend another twenty minutes in my room just staring at the ceiling, but eventually I stop thinking about Brady and Gabe and Elle, and begin thinking about how in the world I am ever going to feel happy again. Brady was a big part of my life and was certainly part of a lot of happy moments, but I never thought of myself as that girl whose whole world revolved around her boyfriend (though I am quickly finding out that a big chunk of mine actually did). Even with Brady I was someone who hung out with friends, was always working on an event for student council, and could spend hours getting lost in the stories the residents of the retirement home told me.

I roll over and pick up my phone, scrolling through my contacts until I find the name I want to call. "Hello."

"Hey, Angie. It's Everly." I hope she can't tell how nervous I am to be reaching out to her as a friend and not on student council business.

"I know. I have you saved as a contact." She giggles softly. "What's up?"

"I was wondering what you're doing later. Maybe we could hang out or something? It's okay if you're busy." I want to make sure to build in an excuse for her.

"Actually, I was just finishing up my homework. Do you want to head over to the mall with me? My mom left me money to buy my shoes for prom. We could grab dinner at the food court."

I'm smiling ear to ear, but I tell myself to tone it down when I answer. "That sounds fun. Thanks." We decide that she will drive and I rush around my room, grabbing my phone and keys before heading out front to wait. I'm a little worried that we won't have anything to talk about and that there will be long moments of silence when we have nothing to say to each other, but I try not to think about it too much.

We don't even make it to the mall before I realize I've been stressing out for nothing. Angie and I talk so much, there isn't even a moment when silence is heard in her small car. I might not have years of history with her, but we actually think a lot alike. By the time we reach the shops, I'm completely comfortable with her. We wander through a few stores until she finds the perfect pair of silver heels to go with her dress.

"Have you thought any more about finding a date? I think you'd have fun and it would help get your mind off things." She hands the salesperson the shoe and tells him her size.

"No. I don't want it to be a blind date, though. Thanks for offering, but I'm just too anxious for something like that." I don't hide my anxiety, but I also don't usually talk about it. I trust her and that's big for me.

"You do what you need to do to enjoy the night." She reaches over and squeezes my arm. "But I think you'll regret it years from now if you don't go. Elle and Brady already made part of your senior year hell, they shouldn't get to ruin prom too." The man returns with a box. "Besides, sometimes it just feels good to get dressed up and put on makeup. It's good for your soul," Angie says, winking at me as she slides on the heels and takes a practice strut around the store. I watch her, envious of the confidence she has that allows her to walk proudly like a model while wearing rolled-up yoga pants and an oversized T-shirt that hides her petite body. When she twirls around in front of the mirror I laugh.

After leaving the store, we wander into the newly constructed food court. The old days of drab brown and beige tile and small family fast-food stands are behind us. The new layout features bright white walls, succulents hanging from their wall-mounted gardens, and gourmet food packaged quickly for our convenience. The natural light shines in from the big windows all around us. I close my eyes for a second, just enjoying the moment, when Angie's number is called and she leaves to fetch her food from the counter.

"So what do you usually do after school?" Angie asks when my pizza is finally ready and we've found a spot to eat.

"I volunteer at a home for seniors a few times a week. I'm also on the peer mediation team, and there are meetings once a month after school. Other than that I just do homework, try to keep up with the school activities calendar, and on days when I have time before it gets dark I like to run."

"Do you like being a peer mediator? I can't imagine listening to all the drama." She flicks her wrist.

"I do, actually. I like getting to the bottom of things and seeing that there is a solution. I don't like it when we are dealing with a bully. I can usually tell within the first ten minutes if we're going to be able to reach an understanding or if it's going to have to be sent further up the chain of command and need an adult to step in. What about you? What are you usually doing after school?" I ask, taking a bite of my pizza.

"I babysit. I have a neighbor down the street who has two little boys. When she has a day that she needs to stay late in the office or if she just wants to go to the gym or to her book club, she calls me. It's easy work and I get money to live on for the month. There are some things I want to do before we graduate and having a little cash will help with that."

"Like what?" I shake my cup, helping my straw settle to the bottom so I can get a large sip.

"I want to take some sort of self-defense class. I know a lot of people look at me and assume I can't defend myself because of my size, so I want to have the skills to prove them wrong. I hope I never have to use it, but since I'll possibly be walking across a dark campus in the fall, it wouldn't hurt to know a few moves." She twirls her noodles around her fork and takes a dainty bite.

"I've always wanted to take a class like that. I think a small studio just opened up by my house. I've seen a lot of women leaving the class all sweaty but smiling like they enjoyed it. Maybe we should check it out some time."

"Are you serious? That would be so fun!" She practically beams with excitement. "Also, I've been meaning to ask you, do you want to help out with the senior prank?"

"I didn't peg you as a prankster. What's the plan so far?"

I'm pretty sure that she has never gotten in trouble, in any area of her life. I can't imagine her taking part in something that could prevent her from walking at graduation. She just smiles at me and shrugs one shoulder coyly.

"I'm going out with a bang. What can they do to me? I have a clean record. I don't think they'd really throw the book at me if I get caught." She takes a sip of her drink and then leans in to tell me the plan. "We're going to turn quad four into a beach party."

"How are you going to do that?" I love the idea.

"Well, *we* are going to bring in sand and some blow-up pools. A few of us have been texting back and forth about it. Our first real meeting to discuss the details is next Friday at lunch. You have to come. We need all the help we can get to make it epic!" I'm nodding my head before she can even finish. I already have a million ideas of things that we can do to make the prank legendary, but then I remember that Brady and Elle will probably be there too. She must see the fear pass over my face because she quickly adds, "It's just a small group of seniors right now. We aren't going to open it up to more students until it gets closer to make sure no one spills the beans to the wrong person."

"Okay, I'm in."

"What about you, is there anything left on your senior year bucket list?"

I take a minute to think about her question. Now that the relationship fog is clearing, I'm finally looking at the end of my senior year with fresh eyes. I haven't been planning anything because I've been so wrapped up thinking about what could have been with Brady. Angie is reminding me that there is a whole world of experiences left that have nothing to do with being a couple. "I want to play on the senior girls powderpuff team."

Angie practically drops her next bite of food. "Really? You know that some of the football boys coach, right?" Her expression shows concern.

"I know." I offer a tight smile. Even though as secretary of activities I am responsible for planning the game, I had been reluctant to sign up for that very reason. But I didn't want to keep letting my fear of seeing Brady prevent me from doing things I liked. And I'd been excited about playing in it since my freshman year.

"We should start working on it and see how you feel when the time comes." I think that's what I love most about Angie—the way she encourages me to go out on a limb, but doesn't shove me off of it. I can't put off planning it much longer. The game is played as part of the senior games during our spirit week, and if we don't get started, we won't have enough kids signed up to make it a success.

"Sounds good." It will be so fun to see what position

each of my friends choose to play. As I imagine who might be up for it, I make sure to carve out a place specifically for Angie. "We'll need a cornerback."

Angie pretends to examine her small frame. "Looks like I'm the girl for the job." We both laugh before finishing our dinners. I've been sitting back waiting for all these senior moments to pass by; maybe having a hand in them will help me feel more in control.

twelve

MONDAY MORNING I pull my car into an open spot in
the row reserved for seniors. I stayed up late last night writing down a few ideas for spirit week and creating a tentative
schedule. I'm early this morning because I want to have time
to ask Mrs. Cramier a few questions before school starts. I
think I have all the details I'm going to need to get student
council's backing, but I can't be sure until I run it past her.
I'm a little anxious that I won't be able to pull everything
together to make this year's spirit week something special
the seniors will always remember.

A knock on my window startles me and my hand flies to

my chest to help hold my heart so it doesn't pound right out of my skin. Gabe is outside my passenger window, trying not to laugh as I take big breaths. "Sorry," he says quickly when I narrow my eyes at him. Those self-defense classes will hopefully teach me how to not jump out of my skin at a moment's notice. I hit the button to put down the window, but instead of leaning in to talk to me he lifts the small knob and unlocks the door. He's sitting beside me so quickly it makes me smile.

"Good morning," I say, turning in my seat so that I can look at his amused expression.

"You're a bit jumpy." He leans back against the seat and grins at me. Even if I wanted to be mad at him for the possible heart attack, I just can't seem to muster the anger when he's looking at me with that charming expression. "I saw your car and thought I'd say hello." He puts the window up again so the students passing by can't hear our conversation.

"Hello," I reply with a small laugh, finally letting my hand on my chest fall to my lap.

Gabe is looking around my car, taking in the radio station I'm listening to and the small charm that hangs from my rearview mirror. I forgot to take it down after the breakup. It's Brady's football number. Gabe holds it in his palm long enough to lean forward and study it before letting it go again. I reach for it and lift it from the mirror, letting it gather on my palm. Gabe watches me silently, but I don't feel like he's making any judgments. I feel a little embarrassed that it was forgotten until just now. Gabe takes it from my hand and opens my glove box, then he places it carefully inside and shuts the door.

We both stare straight out the windshield and watch as a few kids make their way out of the parking lot. It feels unsettling to have that charm in this small space with us. I suddenly want it gone, because it feels like it has the power to suffocate me just by being in my space. I move quickly, leaning across his legs to pop open the glove box, and grab the unlucky charm. I grip it in my fist and look for a place to get rid of it. Gabe is watching me curiously and as my eyes find their way to the large hedge outside his window, he turns to follow my gaze.

"Looks like you found it a good home," he says reassuringly, lowering the window on his side. He doesn't make another move. When I pull my arm back his smile grows and he leans back to clear a path. My heartbeat picks up again, my blood moving quickly through my veins, making my head feel a little dizzy. Everything else that once belonged to Brady I packed up nicely and had my sister return to him.

"Thank you," I say after I let the charm fly and watch it fall into a dark hole in the old shrubbery. Gabe leans out the window to see where it landed, but it's no use. I watched it sail into the darkness and get lost forever. It feels . . . better.

His light chuckle fills the car as he puts the window back up. "It's against the law to have your view restricted," he says, overly serious, as if I might have needed a good excuse for losing my mind momentarily.

"I've had my view restricted for a very long time." I sigh and lean back in my seat. I don't clarify what I mean because he must already know that I'm not talking about the charm anymore.

"Should we burn some sage or something?" he asks, dipping his chin and twisting his head so he can look at me. I can't help but laugh. I'd never tell him that the thought had crossed my mind. How easy it would be if we could just burn some sage and smoke out all the old feelings.

"Maybe." I turn my head and meet his gaze. I wonder if I shouldn't be this vulnerable in front of him, but I can't help it. I've never been good at hiding how I feel and something about Gabe makes me want to confide in him. Gabe nods his head and looks around. He opens the door and steps up out of his seat. I watch him reach through the open window of the car next to us and grab the tree air freshener hanging on the rearview mirror. He dips back in and shuts the door.

"Close enough." He pulls the tree completely from its package and my car is quickly filled with the overwhelming fragrance of a fresh-cut pine tree. "I'm not sure what we're supposed to say." He lets the tree dangle from its small loop.

"I didn't look that far into it," I admit with a shrug.

"What's your favorite song?" His question takes me by surprise and I look into his eyes as I think about my answer. He waits patiently for me. "You can be honest. I won't make fun of you," he teases. The thought hadn't crossed my mind. A boy who goes out of his way to comfort a girl in the bathroom and then also steals an air freshener just to make her smile doesn't seem like a guy who would be mean about musical preferences.

"'Nobody to Blame,' by Chris Stapleton, feels like a good fit." I have a broad taste in music. I love many things, from rock to country. He gives me a supportive nod.

"It's an outstanding fit." He presses his back against his seat and lifts his hips, twisting a little so he can grab something out of his pocket. I laugh as he balances the tree and pries his phone from his pants. He holds it up for me to see before sitting back down and scrolling through it. He watches my face as the song starts to play. My heart warms as he nods his head to the beat.

"I wouldn't have guessed you like country music," I say, loud enough for him to hear over the song.

"Are you kidding?" he asks, drawing his brows together. "I like all good music. Rap, rock, country, oldies." He sets his phone on my dash and holds the tree for me to take. I laugh and shake my head, too shy to take it from him. He tilts his head to the side and moves the tree a little closer. His smile is even bigger than it was a minute ago and it feels infectious. My cheeks hurt from how big mine grows. When I cover my face and shake my head, he uses his free hand to pull my hands away. He waves the air freshener around, making sure to clear the air in every corner he can reach.

"People will think you're crazy," I warn as a few kids pass in front of us.

"People will think what they want to think, Everly. It's human nature to fill in the gaps. Do you think I'm crazy?" he asks as he scrunches his nose up and makes a big show out of rubbing the tree along the mirror where the charm had been hanging. The fresh smell is becoming overwhelming, but he carries on like the most important thing is finishing his mission to rid my car of bad Brady energy.

He dangles the tree in front of me again and this time I pull it from his finger. "No, but I probably should. You're helping me sage my car with a pine-scented air freshener you stole from that other car." I'm laughing again as I roll my eyes and wiggle the tree in the corner nearest me. I know it isn't sage, and we aren't really doing anything ritualistic to force out the bad energy, but it feels like it's working somehow. I'm laughing and the weight of the breakup is forgotten for a moment as Gabe points out a few places that I've missed with the tree.

Our laughing starts to turn into coughing when the fragrance overwhelms us. Gabe takes the air freshener from my hand and tucks it back into the plastic wrap. He opens his door again and sticks his hand through the open window of the car next to us to put it back where it was. When he returns to his seat I give him a curious look.

"What?" he asks nonchalantly, as if this whole experience is totally normal.

"You put it back?!" I wave my hand in front of my face to try to get fresh air. We both reach for our window buttons and open the windows so we don't suffocate from the pungent smell.

"I might be crazy, but I'm not a thief!" he answers as we both laugh, sucking in the fresh air.

We don't get a chance to calm down before the bell rings. "Oh, shit!" I hiss, reaching behind my seat to grab my backpack and then hurrying to put up our windows. Gabe jumps out and I emerge from my side of the car, along with a cloud of pine-scented air. Where did the time go? He's just so easy to be around, it slipped right by. We run through the parking lot, laughing while cutting between the cars and avoiding the parking blocks. We slide to a stop at the street that runs between the parking lot and the high school. Gabe reaches out to pull my arm as soon as there is a break in the traffic.

We are in a full sprint as we pass the old woman who locks the gates, barely making it in before she shuts them behind us with a loud clank and a disapproving shake of her head. "See you later!" Gabe yells as he takes the stairs of building four two at a time and I slip into class just as the final bell rings.

thirteen

THE NEXT DAY Angie slips into her seat beside me during student council. I smile at her and slide the paper I've been writing notes on into the center of the table so she can read it. Her eyes move quickly as she scans the sheet. "It's just a few ideas," I say as I wait for her to finish. The other student council members are moving around the room, working independently on activities. Angie smiles and looks over her shoulder to make sure no one is watching us.

"These are great ideas!" she whispers with excitement. I pull the paper back and fold it up. I was bored in my second period class so I spent some time thinking about what we might need to help transform the quad into a beach. I feel like I've been dragging along most days, but when I started the list I felt invigorated. It seemed to spark something inside me and once I got going, coming up with ideas was a breeze.

"I'm just not sure how we'll get enough sand." It would be too expensive to buy, and I'm sure there are rules about taking it from the beach.

"Kathy has a hookup. Her dad is in construction or something and she said she can get a ton of it pretty easily. Do you really think we can get a palm tree?" She giggles, referring to the small drawing I had made at the bottom of my notes.

"I think it would be awesome it we could. I'm not too sure about the logistics of it just yet, but imagine how funny it would be if it was standing tall right in the middle of the quad. I also checked Craigslist and found a few grills and old ice chests for reasonable amounts. We won't want anything they can trace back to us, but the bigger the objects, the harder it will be for them to get it cleared up before anyone can see."

Angie nods her head and grabs her phone from her pocket. She quickly begins to type. "I'm going to start a new group text so you can see what we are working on and add your ideas so the other people can see them." My phone buzzes in my pocket as she hits send.

Mrs. Cramier steps into the room and I slip the folded

piece of paper into my backpack. Usually she spends the days we don't have meetings scheduled in her office, trusting us to be working on what we are assigned. Once in a while she pops over to make sure we are focused, or to tell us something. She glances around the room and when she makes eye contact with me, she smiles and heads in my direction.

"Everly, I wanted to talk to you for a minute." She pulls up a chair to the opposite side of the table. "You too, Angie." Angie and I glance at each other quickly and I wonder if her heart is beating as quickly as mine. I'm so grateful the evidence of the senior prank planning is safely tucked away in my bag.

"Sure," I say as casually as possible.

"I spoke with Coach Carter about the powderpuff game. He assured me he would find two responsible boys to help coach the girls." She smiles at us and I feel my stomach twist and then shove itself up beneath my ribs. My hands get sweaty and I start to get that out-of-body feeling. *Please don't say Brady.*

"That's great," Angie says. Her eyes meet mine and I can see the concern in them. I try to smile, but I'm sure I fail. "Did he say who it would be?" She gives me a tight smile before turning her attention back to Mrs. Cramier.

"He did." I'm waiting on her next words like a defendant waits for the judge to hand down their sentence. I'll be fine no matter who she names, but if it's Brady there's a huge chance my experience won't be as fun as I was hoping it could be. She sits back in her chair and I get the feeling she might have heard about what's been happening between Brady, Elle, and me. Everyone is talking about it after all, and Mrs. Cramier is a student favorite when it comes to cool teachers.

"I suggested that maybe this year he could choose boys who aren't always in the spotlight. It might be fun for them to get a chance to show students what they can do." Her words sink in through the fog of my anxiety and I let out the air that had been trapped in my lungs. She leans forward slightly, making the conversation between the three of us feel private and significant. "I think it's important that the student coaches have great ethics, don't you?"

There is no doubt now that she knows about everything. She reaches out and squeezes my wrist before standing up. "Thank you," I manage to say as I look up at her. Her support slightly eases the hurt in my heart.

She nods her head. "You have too much going for you to get bogged down by anyone who doesn't treat you with the same respect you treat them. Enjoy your game, Everly. I'm sure Ethan and Hector will be wonderful coaches." She turns and heads back into her office, leaving Angie and me speechless. After a full minute of trying to convince myself that the whole conversation really happened, I turn to Angie and see her smiling. She opens her arms and gives me a big hug.

"I told you it would work out!" she says, and for the first time I'm convinced it really will. We spend the rest of class discussing the game and working out a practice schedule with the secretary of sports. We managed to have a tentative plan figured out by the time the final bell rings, and I leave class to head to counseling happy, hopeful, and excited, knowing the day is only going to get better when I see Gabe before my appointment.

This time Gabe beats me to the waiting room. When I swing open the heavy glass door, I find him sitting on our usual couch, two large white takeout cups in his hands. I smile when our eyes meet and he hands me a warm cup as I sit down next to him. "I wasn't sure if you liked coffee so I got hot chocolate instead."

"Thanks." The warm drink feels good and calms my stomach. I haven't really eaten all day and it isn't until this moment that I realize just how hard it's been to relax and enjoy something. I hand him his hoodie and the book he lent me. He sets them on top of the notebook in his lap. "I'm almost sad to give that book back to you," I say.

His lips curl into a smile and he taps the cover. "It's one of my favorites. My sister convinced me to read it about a year ago, and as soon as I finished it I had to read his other novels."

"Does she go to our school?"

"She did. Maggie graduated two years ago." He keeps his eyes on his lap and runs a hand over his short hair.

"I don't know many people from that graduating class. Her name doesn't sound familiar, but I also don't know your last name." I'm almost embarrassed to admit it, but the words tumble out of my mouth.

"Darcy." His eyes meet mine and it seems like he is waiting for some sort of recognition, but it doesn't help me remember her. I shrug my shoulders and take another sip of the hot chocolate. His chest deflates with the breath he was holding and he looks up to the ceiling for a second before crossing one leg over the other, resting his ankle on his thigh, and turning toward me. "She was on the cross-country team. Got a full ride to Berkeley."

"Wow, that's really impressive. I like to run, too. I haven't been doing much of it lately, but even when I was jogging regularly I can't imagine being fast enough for a scholarship!" I turn to face him and the conversation suddenly feels more intimate.

"What about you? Do you have any siblings?"

"Rosie. She's a sophomore. Cheers for the JV squad." He nods his head and takes a drink. The nosy lady from last week pushes open the glass door and takes her seat across from us. She gives me a small smile before pulling a magazine from her tote bag. I wonder if she will actually read it this time or if she's planning on listening to the latest development in our budding friendship.

Gabe looks over to the woman and then lowers his voice. "I meant to ask you this yesterday, how did the rest of your afternoon go after you left campus on Friday?"

"Peachy." My answer earns me a small chuckle. "Did everyone talk about it all afternoon?" I hate that my voice sounds desperate, but I know he'll tell me the truth.

"Until lunch, but then Aaron Sharpner bought his date a puppy and smuggled it onto campus with this enormous bow on its neck and that became the lead story."

"You can't be serious. A puppy?" I shake my head in disbelief, both that Aaron would do that and that somehow I hadn't heard about it—probably because Jonathan Little managed to round up the drama club and organize a flash mob in the parking lot after school on Monday to ask his date. Apparently that made the puppy promposal old news.

"A puppy with a red bow. I gave him a few points for picking a traditionally romantic color." This time I laugh and the woman across from us tips her magazine down and leans forward as if it will help her hear us better. I give her my best are-you-kidding-me glare before turning back to Gabe.

"I feel bad for your gender," I tease.

"Why's that? If you tell me it's because we have no idea how to be romantic, I'd like to point out that Jack Messer brought a small folding table and pulled off a candlelit lunch for Tanya Bisbee before the lunch ladies got on his case about having fire at school." He lifts his brows, daring me to argue about the romanticism. I giggle and shake my head.

"I believe boys know how to be romantic. I just think it's unfair that the pressure is always on you guys to do the asking. I heard nineteen ninety-eight was the first year they let a same-sex couple go to prom together. It's been decades. You'd think we could progress in our gender expectations and see more girls asking boys." I'd never be brave enough, but I know a few girls who would be.

"It certainly would make things more interesting." He turns his body even more in my direction. One of his strong arms rests on the back of the couch. Gabe is confident, and I admire that. "So," he says with a smirk, "how would you do it?"

My heart speeds up a little with excitement. I squint my eyes and let out a big sigh, pretending to think hard about what I might do. I've never thought about it. "See what I'm talking about?" I fan my face playfully. "There's so much pressure." He chuckles and rests his head against his hand.

"I've got a few minutes. You can't do any worse than bad eighties remix."

"I guess it would depend on who I was asking. I think the best ones are the invites that aren't as impressive to us on the outside, but mean something to the inviter and invitee."

He nods his head. "True. I hate being embarrassed in front of large groups of people. I don't know if I'd ever have the guts to put myself out there with some cheesy gimmick to try to convince a girl to go to a dance with me. But I have to admit, the ones that are from the heart and clearly mean something to the couple get to me. I find myself rooting for the guy instead of shaking my head and wondering what website he stole the script from."

Add charming and funny to the list of things I'm finding I like about Gabe.

"I feel the same way. I've been avoiding the videos people are putting up on social media, but every once in a while if one looks like it's creative and not just some cookie-cutter idea stolen from the internet, I can't help but click and watch it." I guess deep inside my heart there were still a few cells that lit up for romantic gestures. Maybe one day someone would help me nurture that part of myself, but for now it was enough to know it was there.

"You can't be that good at predicting video gold." Gabe narrows his eyes at me with suspicion. "You must have seen something terrible by accident at least once."

"It really is unfortunate that you can't unsee what you've seen on the internet." I shake my head to try and dissuade him from asking me to elaborate.

"Well," he says with a large exhale of air, "now you have to tell me all about it."

"Fine. But don't say I didn't try to warn you. The video was titled 'Tattooed on My Heart.'" I bring my hands together to form a heart with my fingers. His smile is so warm it's as if I can feel it in my chest as he watches me. "I fell for the title. It wasn't a kid from our school; it was some school back east I think. The guy was wearing a sweater and it was all going so well until all of a sudden it wasn't."

"Why is your face all scrunched up like that?" He chuckles quietly at my grossed-out face. I wish I could erase the image from my mind, but sadly I'm certain it will be there forever.

"He said all these beautiful things to her." I continue with the story, remember how I'd watched the girl's smile grow with each compliment he gave her.

"Sounds like he was doing all right so far."

"Then he took off his sweater and had the word 'prom' shaved into his overgrown chest hair." I try not to laugh again as I tap my heart and raise my brows. "Over his heart."

"You're making that up." His face is serious and I bite my

lip so I don't laugh too loudly.

"I'm not." I pull out my phone and search for the video online. It only takes a minute to bring it up and play it for Gabe.

"I'm going to have to spend this whole session working on how to get that image out of my head," he says when the video is over.

"That was the highlight of my day," I reply with a grin. "Laughter is clearly the best therapy." He runs his hand over his head again and smiles at me. I think about asking him if we could hang out some time without the old busybody, but the words don't find their way out of my mouth before his therapist opens his office door and calls to him.

"Good luck in there," I tease.

"I'm starting to repress it already." He's on his feet and out of sight, and before regret for my missed opportunity can really sink in, Laura opens her door. I make my way to her office with the first few symptoms of disappointment beginning to weigh on me.

"How are you, Everly? Anything new?" She sits down in the chair across from me, and I toss my empty cup into her trash before reaching for my favorite pillow and pulling it onto my lap, kicking off my flip-flops, and tucking my feet underneath me.

"I was pretty much pushed from my *staircase of fear.*"

Her lip twitches like she wants to laugh but instead she holds it together. "What do you mean?" She twirls her pen between her fingers.

"You told me to think of my biggest fear and I chose Brady asking Elle to prom as the top step. I thought we would have time to baby-step our way up, and you could give me some coping tools to use along the way. Of course, that's not how it worked out. I walked out of my third period class on Friday and right into my worst nightmare." I pick at the seam on the edge of the overstuffed pillow. She waits for me to continue.

"It was tacky and cheesy and completely over the top, but I wasn't ready for it. I lost it. I ran for the girls' bathroom again, but someone stopped me instead."

"A friend of yours?"

I shake my head but then nod. "I don't know. I think so." I tip my head in the direction of the office next door. "It was the guy, Gabe, from the waiting room. He pulled me into the boys' room so the girls wouldn't see me cry. Then he helped to sneak me out the visitors' gate so I wouldn't have to go back to class."

Laura offers an empathetic smile. "What did it feel like to have someone care about your feelings?"

"I think it helped. My mom and sister have been trying to comfort me, but sometimes that makes me feel worse.

They worry so much about me and I feel like I need to reassure them I'm going to be okay. I can't just let it out."

"With Gabe you can?"

"I guess. He helped me and then he made me laugh." I feel my cheeks burn a little with embarrassment.

"Sounds like he's a good person to be around."

"Does it?"

"You do a lot for other people." She flips open my chart and lifts up a few pieces of paper. "You volunteer, you've mentored for the middle school girls, and just a few months ago you received that award for completing sixty hours of peer mediation. You're a strong, amazing young woman. It's wonderful that someone wanted to do something nice for you."

I can't help but blush a little at her compliment. I don't do those things for the recognition, I do them because it makes me feel like I can make a difference, even if that difference might be small.

"So what is your big fear now? You thought the invite would kill you, but you survived. It hurt and you cried, but then you kept breathing." She slowly closes my file and shuffles her notebook up to the top of the stack resting in her lap.

"I kept breathing but I ditched school. It's not the best option, and if it keeps happening my parents are going to get pissed." I toss the pillow aside and stretch my feet out on her ottoman.

"No, not the best option, but an option nonetheless. Think of this as somewhat of a crisis mode you're in. You knew your limits and you left. Next time maybe you'll be able to stay." She writes a quick note and then returns her gaze to me.

"My new fear is that I'll never have my life back. I want to feel normal again. I want to smile just because, and not worry that my next big heartache is waiting around every corner. I want to look forward to things again and eat without it feeling like a chore. Does it ever get better?"

"That's a trick question. Yes and no. One day you will smile again, you'll stop looking over your shoulder waiting for something bad to happen, and you'll look forward to eating again, but you will never be the same as before. You won't want to be. You have learned so many lessons from your time with Brady and this breakup. You've learned how to love and be loved, how to commit to someone, and how to survive when that person betrays you. Those are things you will never want to unlearn. They have become a part of you. One day you will feel better and be better, but you will also be different."

I nod my head and feel my lips curve into a smile. That sounds perfect. I just hope she can get me there soon.

"Give me a fear we can overcome, a place where you want to be."

"I want to go to prom and have a good time." The words slip quickly from my mouth.

"That's great! Let's build your staircase and see if we can make some progress." She hands me a blank sheet of paper on a clipboard and has me quickly draw a staircase.

"Okay, put your biggest fear on the top step." I follow her instructions and write *Experience senior prom without Brady* in big, bold letters. "Now we just need to work our way up to that. What sounds slightly less scary than the completion of your senior prom without him? Like it would be the step just below."

"Slow dancing with someone. It's been so long since I danced that close with anyone other than Brady." I look to Laura for her approval. She gives me a knowing smile and points to the paper. I write *Slow dance with new guy* on the step below.

"Now what's just below that?"

This time I don't even have to think much about it. "Pictures. They seem so permanent." I don't wait for her this time, just quickly fill in *Prom pics without Brady*. On the step below I write *Awkward family photos*. I write *Invite* on the bottom step.

"Let's set a time frame for this step. Without a deadline it's a dream, not a goal."

"If I don't get asked by the Monday before prom, I will

ask someone." Just the thought tightens my stomach and makes me feel a rush of adrenaline.

"I'm going to hold you to that." I know she will remind me, but actually making this goal happen is completely on me. I keep my Tuesday slot for next week when we schedule my appointment, and Laura lightly pats my back as I leave, telling me that she's proud of the work I've done so far.

As I go back into the waiting room I see that Gabe is walking out of his therapist's office. I don't look back at Laura, but I can feel her watching as he opens the glass door and waits for me to go through.

fourteen

THE PARKING LOT is thinning out as we walk down the front steps of the building together. When we reach the last step, I look up at him and smile, curious about what to do next. Is he walking me to my car or are we going to separate here? As the thought floats around in my head, a nervous butterfly feeling begins to swoosh around in my gut.

"Do you need to go home right now?" I ask him. I see his eyes look away from mine quickly and return with a grin that seems to tip unevenly on one side. He's nervous too, the air between us seeming to grow thick as I wait for his answer.

"No. I just need to be back by eight." We have about three hours, and I'm pretty excited at the idea that I could get to spend them with him. After the fun I had last Friday with Angie I realized what a mistake it was to close myself off to the possible friendships around me, and I don't want to miss this chance to get to know Gabe better. "We could hang out for a little bit if you're up for it." His hand moves to the back of his head, where he slides it over his bristly hair.

"Okay."

"Yeah?" He seems surprised. I laugh and nod my head. "Cool. Are you hungry? We could grab something to eat." I'm never hungry anymore, but I don't tell him that right now because I am dying to spend more time with him. I quickly text my mom to let her know I'm out with a friend and I won't be home until curfew.

"Sure."

Gabe points to his truck in the corner of the parking lot. "I'll drive." We weave our way through the few scattered cars and he clicks the key fob, unlocking the door for me, but still moves to the passenger side to open it. I climb up and buckle my seat belt as he shuts the door and walks around the truck. Once he's buckled in he fires up the engine and music fills the cab.

I've never heard the song that is playing, but immediately my body wants to move with the beat. I don't, of course—that would make him think I was totally crazy—but I lean over a little to see if his stereo display will tell me the name of the singer. "You can change it if you want," he says when he catches me looking at the screen.

"I like it. I've just never heard it before. Who sings this?"

"Ed Sheeran." He turns up the volume and waits a minute so I can hear the chorus. The singer's thick accent makes it hard to understand the words at times, especially when they're sung quickly, but I love it. The passionate voice contrasting with the smooth sound of the guitar chords seems to resonate in my chest.

Gabe is watching me and he turns the volume back down slightly so he can talk. "I saw him in concert once. Maggie wanted to go and somehow talked me into coming along even though I thought I would be the only guy in a sea of twelve-year-old girls. There *were* a lot of middle school girls, but there were a lot of guys there, too." He puts the truck in reverse and throws his arm across the back of the seat so he can look behind us as he pulls out. It occurs to me then that I want him to touch me again, which I realize isn't exactly something I'd want from a friend, but I quickly dismiss the thought. His hand feels so near to my skin and yet so far away at the same time.

"I've never been to a concert." His eyes flash to mine and a look of disbelief crosses his features.

"Never? Not even an embarrassing boy band or screechy pop diva?"

"No," I say, laughing. "I love music, I guess I just never had any one particular group or singer I felt like I had to see live. Was it fun?"

"It was great. He plays with a loop station. It's incredible to watch. It's just this guy with his guitar, a microphone, and this machine. He walks out onto the stage and plays the first layer of music, the steady background guitar rhythm, and he records it. Then he plays the next layer, then his background singing. Finally when all the layers are playing together, he jams out on his guitar and sings like it's the easiest thing in the world, only you know it can't be. He's the entire band." We are stopped at the edge of the parking lot, and I can see how impressed he is by the way his eyes widen and his hands mimic playing the guitar as he walks me through the steps.

"Sounds like I missed a good show."

"You have to see it," he says adamantly. When I give him a small nod he asks, "What sounds good to eat?"

"Honestly?" I ask on a sigh, leaning back into the seat. I look at the side of his face, the way his dark eyelashes frame his unique eyes and his strong jaw creates a sleek line against the smooth skin of his neck. He's so different from Brady, and I wonder if that is adding to his allure.

He looks left and then right, past my face so he can catch

the break in traffic. Once we pull onto the road he looks back to me. "Honestly." My eyes drift down to his lips and then back to his eyes.

"I haven't really been excited about food lately." His single nod lets me know he understands, and I turn my head back to look out the front windshield. Maybe it's because I know he's in therapy too, or maybe it's because of how he was when he comforted me in the bathroom, but I don't feel like I have to pretend with him. My mom would pat my hand and my sister would launch into some pep talk about needing to move on and not let them have this power over me. I wait for him to jump in with some sort of intervention, but refreshingly he just listens.

We pull into the parking lot of a little ice cream shop. He parks us right in front and then cuts the engine. "How about a shake?" My eyes drop to where his hand is now resting on the seat between us.

"I could do a shake." I can't remember the last time I had one. My stomach seems to wake up a little at the idea and, if I focus hard, I can feel the small pang of hunger.

We go inside and order our shakes, which Gabe pays for, but instead of sitting at one of the tables inside we get back into the truck. "I want to show you something. Do you want to go for a little ride?" he asks.

I nod my head, afraid to open my mouth and allow him

to hear the excitement in my voice. Getting to know him is exhilarating. I don't ask where we're going now as he sips his shake and pulls back out onto the road. It doesn't matter; I just want to be in his company.

"I have a few more books for you if you're interested." He leans back against his seat as we drive down the small road.

"Sounds like you read a lot. Do you read different genres or do you have a favorite?" I ask.

"It's funny you ask that; I used to read only nonfiction. My favorite books were autobiographies of sports legends or war heroes. But then my family went through a bit of a tough time, and I found myself picking up fiction instead. I guess it felt like more of an escape or something. I used to think it was a waste of time. I'm not big on pretending, but I've found that sometimes authors can tell a story so convincingly that you have to keep reminding yourself it's not true."

"I know! I had to remind myself of that when I finished the book you gave me. If I didn't have that to hold on to I would have been a crying mess." I take another sip of my shake as Gabe laughs.

"I would never get emotional over a book," he says jokingly and I laugh at the expression on his face. I'm glad to know I'm not the only one who gets swept away by the words on the pages of a great novel.

"What's the worst story you've read?"

I hesitate to tell him because I wonder what he'll think of me. "I'm embarrassed to share," I finally admit.

"Don't tell me you read fanfiction about Justin Bieber. I'll have to make you walk back to the office," he teases.

"No." I shake my head and chuckle. "I read a lot of romance novels on my Kindle." I crinkle my nose and eyes as I wait for his judgment.

"My sister loves reading romances. You guys could probably have a pretty steamy book club if you ever met. Tell me about the bad one."

I feel my shoulders relax. I've never met a boy who could talk books the way he can. Brady didn't like reading and used to get irritated when I wanted to tell him about something I'd read. He once made fun of a romance novel he found on my Kindle and ever since then I've been deleting them the minute I finish the story. "It was a story that hooked me with the blurb. It was a romance and the characters were young. I like stories where I can relate."

Gabe is smiling and sneaking glances at me when it's safe. He's clearly interested in what I'm saying so I push on. "I loved the first five chapters. The main character was falling for this intriguing guy. They go on a few dates and then just when it starts to get interesting, they both die and become vampires."

Gabe laughs out loud. "Vampires?"

"Stupid, stupid, vampires!" I laugh. "Look, I don't judge people who are into that. I get that some girls love the idea of sexy vampires falling for humans, but I don't want to read it myself. I feel like that little fact should have been mentioned in the blurb."

"That's awful."

"You're telling me! I was already invested in the characters. I had given that author a few hours of my free time and then she clubbed me over the head and dragged me off in a direction I didn't want to go."

"What do you mean she dragged you off . . . you finished it!" He points at me when he assumes correctly that I couldn't let the story go without reading until the end. "Really, Everly?" he teases. "I never pictured you as a fang chaser." I open my mouth in pretend offense, but laughter tumbles out after just a second. I close my eyes and push my head back against the headrest. We are both laughing hard now, and my free hand moves over my stomach. The muscles are sore after just a few minutes because I haven't laughed that hard in a long time.

"My sister made me read the Twilight series," he admits when we are finally calming down, and that gets us started again.

"She *made* you?"

"Okay, maybe just the first one. But I had to know how it ends. If you tell another soul my secret I'm going to deny it."

I'm smiling so big my cheeks hurt as I cross my heart with my finger. The road wraps around behind large office buildings and a few department stores. Gabe tells me about a famous veteran from our hometown who flew airplanes in World War II. The small airport at the end of the road is named after him. As we bounce over a few of the worn patches of pavement I notice his notebook on the floor between us. I wonder what his therapy homework is and if he's been in counseling for a long time. I pull the cold, thick shake into my mouth, taking the opportunity to sneak a glance at him while he focuses on the road ahead of us. I'm not sure where he's taking me, but being with him is making me feel better than I have in a long time. Finally he pulls into an empty lot near the airport.

The sun is beginning to dip behind the taller buildings as he backs into a spot near the fence. We get out of the car and move to the back of his truck and he lowers the tailgate, setting his shake on it and then turning to me. There is no way I can get up there. Even with it lowered, the tailgate is well above my waist. I set my shake down next to his, thinking that maybe we are just going to stand here.

The roar of a jet engine grows louder as a private jet taxis down the runway past us. When it lifts up into the air we watch it gain altitude and fly away until the sound is only a faint noise in the distance. I drop my gaze back to Gabe and he holds his hands out. I realize he's offering to lift me up onto the tailgate of his truck and that chivalrous gesture causes a flush to spread across my cheeks and down my neck. His eyebrow rises in question and I nod, accepting his help.

His warm, strong hands are on my hips, the heat of his body close enough for me to soak it up, and the scent of him already familiar as he grips me and lifts effortlessly, setting me down on the tailgate.

He doesn't pull his hands back right away, and I feel my breath catch as I look down into his eyes. It's a completely innocent gesture he's just performed, but now his large, toned body is between my legs, his arms resting on my thighs as he looks up at my face. I wonder if his skin would feel soft around his eyes and scratchy at his chin. His gaze dips down to my lips for a brief moment.

Gabe quickly steps away. The truck shifts for a second as he easily jumps up and takes a seat beside me, handing me my shake from the spot next to him. I lean back on my hand and watch as another plane, this time a small propeller plane, takes off over us. I've lived in this town my whole life and I had no idea this parking lot even existed, let alone the entertainment it provided.

"So what do you do when you're not at therapy or stuck at school?" he asks, his gaze following a plane as it descends from the sky above and lands at the far edge of the airport.

"I volunteer at a retirement home and work on things for student council. Right now with prom coming up there are a lot of little things that have to be taken care of. I also spend time with my sister and my parents."

Gabe drinks the last few sips of his shake and sets his cup aside. "What's it like to volunteer at the retirement home? I haven't been in one since my great-grandmother passed away. I still remember the way the hallway smells."

The sun is beginning to sink toward the horizon, bringing out the beautiful orange-and-rose-colored hues that make the sky look like a painting. "I was a little nervous at first. It's hard to face your own fears head-on. I never want to be confined to a bed or stuck in a wheelchair at the end of my life. It made me really sad to see that some residents don't ever get visitors." I shake my cup and move the straw down to the bottom again to get the last of it. "I look forward to my time there now. I make sure to stop by the rooms of the residents who haven't had any family in for a while. I can tell who they are because the policy is to have visitors sign in at the front desk. I actually feel guilty that I haven't been there in a while with all that I've had going on."

"I'm sure they'll understand. What do you do with

them?" he asks. I set down my cup and lean back on my hand.

"A few of them like to be read to. They have the same books on their side tables for months at a time. It takes a while to get through the story when I'm the only one reading it. Others like to show me pictures of their families or listen to old radio programs on cassette tape." I turn my head to watch him. "What do you do after school—besides spending time in the pool?"

"I have a lot of responsibilities at home." I hear his voice drift off softly. He looks down to our feet for a minute. "I spend time with my family too. It's hard sometimes because both of my parents work really long hours. My mom is an English professor for the community college and my dad is a graphic artist for a video production company."

I feel my skin prickle with goose bumps and shiver. Gabe's voice is deep next to me. "Are you cold?"

I am, but I don't want this time with him to end. "I'm okay. I think it's the shake." I hold it up for him to see it's empty and then set it behind me in the back of his truck. He tosses his cup behind him and then quickly slips his hoodie off, and I feel a small tinge of disappointment when he pulls his shirt back down where it has slipped up.

I realize just sitting next to him makes me feel a bit on edge. My pulse picks up and my stomach grows lighter, as if Gabe has the ability to charge my body with an invisible spark. He's very attractive, and I find myself looking into those beautiful eyes as he hands his hoodie to me. I slip it over my head and feel the warmth still remaining inside from the heat of his body. I rest back on my hands and kick my feet slowly below the tailgate. "Can I ask you something personal?"

He nods his head and looks at me. "Ask me whatever you want," he answers, lying all the way back, folding his hands together behind his head. I pull his hood over my hair and lie back with him, wiggling a little to get comfortable. Our faces are looking up at the beautiful sky above us, our eyes squinting slightly against the glow of the bright setting sun. I tuck an arm behind my head and take a deep breath.

"Why are you in therapy?" I turn my face toward his and he looks into my eyes. The hesitation I sense makes me regret my question. I open my mouth to tell him never mind, but he takes a big breath and starts to talk.

"My sister tried to commit suicide a little over a year ago, and I'm the one who found her." His voice doesn't falter, but the pain is so entwined with his words I ache for him.

The sky above us is empty of planes again and the silence begins to get noisy as I hear my heartbeat in my ears. "I'm sorry, that wasn't my business." I look into Gabe's eyes so he knows I'm being sincere.

"It's not really a secret. A lot of kids at school heard about it." He's watching me now, mirroring my position of resting on one arm, with his face turned in my direction. "She started having a few problems in high school, but my parents thought it was just typical teenage girl behavior.

"Her senior year things got worse, but we just thought she was really stressed. She's a great student and took a full load of AP classes along with running on the cross-country team. She started slipping in the fall, sleeping for days at a time, not being able to get out of bed. My parents thought she was just overdoing it. It didn't feel right, though." His eyes plead with mine to understand, and I give him a small nod. I slip my hand into his and lightly squeeze. "She finally started pulling out of it by the time graduation came around and then during the summer she was unstoppable. We thought she had conquered it."

I tighten my hand in his and he leans closer. "Then she went away to college, and after a few weeks she stopped taking our calls. One night my parents got a call from a social worker at a hospital. My sister had been found by some other students—she'd taken all of her clothes off and was swimming in the pool on campus. She was arrested, but the cops took her to the hospital because she wasn't making any sense."

"That sounds scary, Gabe, what happened?" I lightly

brush my thumb across the top of his hand.

"She was diagnosed with bipolar disorder and put on a pretty rigid regimen of psych meds. She started coming back down to reality and we started to relax again. It was manageable, they told us. She just needed to take her meds." His head shakes a little and he lets out a laugh without humor. "The problem is, once you've felt that high, nothing else feels right. The cycle began to move toward depression, which isn't uncommon as the doctors try to regulate the dose, and she panicked."

He pauses for a moment, lost in thought. I stay silent, hoping he keeps confiding in me. "She was released, but it wasn't good. She withdrew again and had to drop out of her classes for the semester. She came home and just stayed in her room. I tried to get her to go out, but she would tell me she didn't have the energy. She told me once that depression sucked everything from you. She didn't even have the energy to feel sad.

"It was the darkest place she'd ever been, but we all finally started breathing again when she began showing signs of recovering. Now I know that it was that slight recovery that made her feel strong enough to attempt suicide. My parents left for work and she told me she was going to get ready to go running. I smiled . . . I remember it clearly. It was a feeling of relief, like we had made it through again. When she didn't come out of her room before I had to go to school I went to check on her. I found her on her bed in her running clothes. She'd swallowed a bunch of her medications—the empty bottles were lying next to her. There was a letter for us. I wasn't supposed to find her that soon."

I'm not sure what to say, but I know I need to say something. "I can't even imagine that. It must have been horrible. Is she okay now?"

He shrugs his shoulders. "She's stable right now, but I'm still afraid for her. My therapist tells me that it's common for bipolar patients to take themselves off the meds. I guess they think they're better and don't need them anymore, or maybe they miss that feeling of being manic. I'm terrified."

I want so badly to comfort him, but I'm not sure what exactly I should do. He's just shared something so private with me. I pull the hood away from my face so it doesn't look like I'm hiding from him. "I'm so sorry. I love my sister and it would tear me apart to think she might hurt herself. Thank you for sharing with me. I won't tell anyone." I follow my gut and press a kiss to his cheek, hoping it feels as comforting to him as his arms had felt wrapped around me as I cried. When I pull back I can feel the shift in the mood and I can see that some of the worry has left his face.

We sit in friendly silence, watching as every so often a plane takes off in the distance. When a small plane takes off directly above us he asks, "Have you ever been on a plane before?"

"Last summer we flew to Hawaii." I smile at the memory. "It was just the four of us, my parents and sister and me. We rented a house with a pool. It was awesome to spend the day on the beach or exploring the island and then go swimming at night. I can see why you love to swim. I think some of the best times I had on that vacation were swimming in that beautifully clear ocean with my sister."

Gabe nods his head. "Even though I have to swim so often here, I still love getting into some body of water when we're on vacation. There's just something about it that makes me feel relaxed."

"What about you? Have you been on a plane before?"

"Lots of times. My grandparents live in different states. We used to go visit them more when we were younger, but now our family is so busy we only get to see them about once a year. Sometimes I wish I could get on a plane and go somewhere just to go. You know, not have something I have to do there or anyone I have to see. I'd like to get to pick where I'm going too."

"If you could get on a plane tonight, where would you go?" I ask.

"Easy. I would go to a tropical island. Maybe Bora Bora." His face lights up and he turns to look at me. His smile is contagious. "I want to stay in a little hut over the ocean. I love listening to the waves, and I saw this brochure once that showed a hole cut right in the floor of the hut so you can fish or watch the sea beneath you."

"I think I've seen that picture somewhere." I can recall the image of the crystal-blue water. "It sounds amazing."

"You should come with me," he says seriously.

I laugh softly. "To Bora Bora?" It seems so far away and very out of reach for two teenagers in the bed of a truck.

"Hey, no laughing," he teasingly scolds, "it's my pretend vacation. I can invite whoever I want."

"Then I'd love to go."

fifteen

I ALMOST FALL asleep in first period after not getting much rest last night. I lay in bed tossing and turning for hours, feeling a crazy mix of happiness about the amazing time that I had with Gabe last night and frustration that I can't completely let the idea of Brady go. I can't wait for the night that Brady isn't the last thing I think of before falling asleep. I rest my head on my desk, so grateful to be watching a video instead of listening to a lecture. Maybe I can sleep for a little while at lunch today if Rosie doesn't find me.

The bell rings and I slowly trudge away from my desk, feeling like my backpack weighs a million pounds. Prom invitations continue to happen all around me, but the worst is over, so I can appreciate some of the other crazy displays of ingenuity. I turn into my locker bay and stop short when I see Gabe waiting at my locker. His smile is adorable as he dips his chin, perhaps a little embarrassed to have hunted me down.

"Why don't we ever run into each other?" He pushes his shoulder off the locker next to mine and grabs hold of his backpack straps.

I glance around to see who else might be close enough to hear, but I don't see any familiar faces. "That would be because I hide now, and before that I was always tucked into a corner at the lunch benches next to Brady," I say with a little laugh, and twist the dial on my lock, pulling down hard on the metal handle until it opens with a creak. I put away a few of my books, grab my lunch, and then close the old beige door.

"Want some company today? If you'd rather have space that's fine." I feel my stomach flip but can't pinpoint whether the feeling is excitement or anxiety. Since the whole Elle and Brady scandal broke, the three of us have been the hot topic of the school gossip. I've been praying that something else scandalous happens soon so that our story can be old news, but nothing has really happened yet, and I'm so tired of everyone waiting for some new development in our story.

I hate to think how my spending time with Gabe might fuel the fire.

In the end the thrill of having company other than my sister or a paperback wins out. "Company sounds good." I love the smile that stretches across his face.

Gabe motions for me to lead the way and I head to my usual spot, setting my food on the bench and making sure to leave room for him. He sets his bag down, pulls out a sandwich, and digs in.

"I don't remember seeing you at lunch even when I wasn't hiding. Where do you usually eat?" I pull my legs up so I'm sitting cross-legged on the bench.

"I usually swim and then eat later, during my fifth period. It's coach's econ class so he doesn't care." He reaches into his bag and pulls out a sports drink. I twist open the cap of my water and watch a few of the popular boys from my class pass by. They get quiet as they walk past us, but they don't take their eyes off me. I hope they don't make sitting with Gabe into something it's not. I can only imagine how quickly that story would spread once it hit the girls.

"Why does anyone care what I'm doing?" I ask quietly when the boys are finally past us.

"Come on, Everly. You're a pretty girl, and pretty girls don't go unnoticed." He winks and I giggle. "Too cheesy?" he asks playfully.

"Perhaps a bit." I toss a cracker at him and he catches it before it lands and sticks it in his mouth.

"So my sister invited some friends over Saturday for a little barbecue," Gabe says around his mouthful. He chews, swallows, and clears his throat. "If you're free, you should stop by." I move my hand to shade my eyes so I can see his face clearly. He smiles shyly.

"Won't she be mad you invited people to her party?"

He shakes his head. "No, it's not like that with us. We have a lot of friends in common. I think she'd like you." I catch a glimpse over his shoulder of my sister walking toward us. "Besides, I'm manning the grill, so I get to invite whoever I want. Say you'll come."

I take a second to think about what it is I'm agreeing to. My anxiety has been getting a little more manageable these past few days, but the thought of meeting new people at a party seems risky. Maybe I'll have a panic attack in front of all of them. But Laura has told me to at least try to continue doing things even though I feel anxious, because sometimes my brain just needs to see for itself that I'll be fine. Gabe is a lot of fun to be around, and I feel excited about getting to know him better, so I push aside the anxiety and hope it's the right decision.

"I'll come. Thank you."

"Going somewhere fun?" My sister stands above us,

blocking the sun with her body, so I drop my hand. She gives me a curious look. "I was just checking to see if you wanted someone to sit with, but I guess you have that covered?" She looks at Gabe and then back at me.

"You guys should sign up for shifts or something." I roll my eyes at my sister, but deep down I love that she cares enough to at least try to pull me into some sort of social interaction.

"Yeah, we could make up a schedule," Gabe teases. Rosie doesn't get it, but I find it funny. Rosie looks at me, surprised. I guess it's been a while since she's heard me genuinely laugh.

"Okay . . . I'm Rosie, by the way." She looks at Gabe expectantly.

"Gabe."

"I know," she answers. She must see the surprise in my expression because she nervously finishes, "Some of the older girls on the squad talk about you sometimes."

"Cool, Rosie. Way to make it awkward," I say, tossing a cracker at her. She doesn't see it coming, and it bounces off her shoulder and hits the ground in front of us.

Gabe looks back to Rosie. "Mind if I steal her today? I want to pick her brain about a book I'm reading for English. If that is okay with you, Everly," he says, turning back to me. I nod and see relief in my sister's eyes as she adjusts her weight to the other foot, looking over her shoulder for Dawn or some other friend.

"No problem. I'm glad she can put that library in her head to some use. It was nice to meet you, Gabe. I'll catch you later, Everly." Rosie turns around and heads over to a group of girls she knows, and I feel a burden lift from my shoulders.

"Thank you," I say softly to Gabe. "I hate that this stupid breakup is affecting her life. I'm supposed to be the big sister and take care of her, not the other way around. I guess I'm not doing this whole thing right in her eyes."

"I like hanging out with you," he says simply. "As for what you're supposed to be doing, I'm not sure there is a right way to do any of this. There's only trying to be happy. I've learned you should just do what you can to get through the lows so that you can enjoy the highs." His eyes finally leave mine as he reaches for his drink. I know he probably learned that from his sister's experience, and it makes his words feel powerful and sharp. "And being with you is a high for me."

His words make my heart skip a beat. "Try to be happy, huh?" I repeat, skirting around his last sentence as I scoot down and rest my back against my bag. The tired feeling from earlier finds its way back to me. I slip off my Toms and pull my bare feet up to my butt, trying not to crowd him on the bench.

sixteen

I'VE STARTED LOOKING forward to lunch, something I wouldn't have imagined a few weeks ago. Yesterday Gabe and I killed time with a game on his phone. To play, you hold the phone on your forehead facing the other person and they have to give you hints about the word on the screen so you can guess what it is. We giggled through the first category, but once we stumbled upon the Eighties Movies category we couldn't get through our turns without cracking up. Turns out both of our parents have quite a collection of DVDs from that era, which makes us both experts.

"Whose wardrobe does Mr. Vernon raid?" Gabe asked

quickly. He stared at me like the answer should've been easy. I blew a breath and scrunched my face up in thought. Gabe laughs. "Come on! It's one of the best lines in the movie. How do you not remember that?"

"Seriously? Hurry and give me something else!" We forgot that other kids might have been able to hear us, and our voices raised with the excitement of the clock running down. Turns out that Gabe and I share another thing in common. We are both extremely competitive.

Gabe began to sing the first few lines of a famous Barry Manilow song and I knew the answer immediately, but pretended not to remember so he'd keep singing. Finally my smile couldn't be contained and recognition dawned on Gabe's face. "You're totally fucking with me, aren't you?"

"Yes."

"I'll get you back." He grabbed the phone and checked our scores. "How is it possible that our parents both love John Hughes movies?" He tapped the screen a few times and then lifted it to his head as the numbers on the screen counted down from three.

"They're great movies," I answered quickly, looking into his eyes before looking up to read the next word. My eyes grew wide when I saw it and I tried to think of a hint that wouldn't embarrass me. "Um, someone who wants to have sex a lot."

Gabe's smile grew and even though I don't know him that well, I was guessing by the look on his face that he knew the answer. "A teenage boy," he said confidently.

I shook my head. "No, not like that." I playfully slapped his arm. "So much sex that it's too much." I watched the seconds tick away.

"There's never too much sex. You're terrible at this game," he said in a very serious tone. It was then that I realized he was messing with me. I tipped my head to the side and scowled at him. He smiled and said the word very slowly: "Nymphomaniac."

"You're an ass, and that movie is great."

"It's the best," he agreed, taking the phone from his head and handing it back to me. We played a few more rounds and in the end his score was higher, but I didn't care. I would be fine losing to him a million times if it meant he'd spend some of his lunch with me.

I shouldn't be surprised that word of our new friendship has become a hot topic on campus, but it still caught me off guard overhearing two girls discussing the fact that Gabe and I had lunch together twice this week. I might not have noticed Gabe until recently, but clearly other girls had. I've heard a few of the rumors, some of which are true and benign; others are just as vicious and malicious as the ones from before. This week, rumor has it Elle told a few girls on the cheer squad that I probably didn't love Brady at all if I'm already moving on.

When I run into Rosie before lunch on Friday she stops me and asks, "What's going on with you and Gabe?" I just shrug my shoulders. I don't know the answer to that. She smiles at me and I see the relief she feels. "You know what they say," she teases. "The best way to get over someone is to get under someone else." She winks and then quickly adds, "Not that I'd know personally, but I'm almost an expert with everything I hear at cheer practice."

I roll my eyes. "There will be no getting under anyone. For your information I'm not even eating with Gabe today."

"Yeah, but that's just because he's got swim practice. Which, if I were you, I would go watch just to see him in a Speedo." And with another exaggerated wink and a wave Rosie leaves to go join her friends.

While the idea of seeing Gabe in his swimsuit again is a little tempting, I make my way over to Angie and a few of the other girls from student council. She told me that they were going to discuss the senior prank and I should join them. I find her group out on the grass where they usually eat. "Hey, Angie."

"Hi, Everly," she answers, patting the ground beside her. "I'm glad you decided to join us." Lisa and Mandy give me warm smiles. I get the sense that I'm welcome and accepted into their group immediately. I feel a little regret for not trying to sit with them before.

"Thanks for inviting me."

"Anytime!" I open up my sack lunch and start on my sandwich. The girls had been in the middle of a conversation, so they pick it right back up. It's nice to hear about what's happening from a different group of people. When the flow of students walking to lunch dies down and our group is out of earshot from any other group, Angie leans in and says softly, "Let's touch base on the prank."

Kathy starts. "I went to my dad's work yard yesterday. He has four large piles of sand that he hasn't touched in forever. I don't think he will notice at all if we can find a few seniors who drive trucks and are willing to help us get some of it from the yard to school." Kathy looks around the group. "He doesn't work on Sundays, so that would be a good day to do it. We can have everything set up for a Monday before school."

We all smile as our plan comes together. I can practically see the quad filled with sand. "I think we should get together over the weekend and hit up as many garage sales as we can. We should be able to get beach chairs and maybe a few old surfboards or boogie boards," Leticia suggests.

"I can drive us," I offer. The girls nod and I rattle off my cell number when they pull out their phones. We decide

I'll pick everyone up early Sunday morning, and we'll grab coffee before hitting all the garage sales we can find before lunchtime. "I also might have figured out the palm tree. I was listening to Sheila Benson talk about drama club during snack break and remembered the production of *South Pacific* they performed before winter break." The girls seem to perk up with excitement. "That storage room is like a treasure chest full of goodies. They have that huge palm tree along with a couple of inflatable ones."

"That's perfect!" Angie says. "I can talk to her about it next period. We can trust her. She's also the stage manager so she should have the key and probably a ton of ideas. Now that I think about it, I heard she was the set designer for that musical. Maybe she'd like to help organize us on the night we do it."

We all agree and then quiet down as students begin to finish their lunches and walk around. We don't want to risk anyone overhearing our conversation. Our talk turns to graduation and the exciting events most students are looking forward to. I'm starting to get into the spirit, but there are still times I find myself weighed down by the idea of seeing Brady and Elle together at all of them. I shake off the thought and turn my attention back to the group.

"Everyone is talking about spirit week and the senior games," Mandy says. "I tried to check out what you guys have planned for this year, but there was such a big crowd around the sign-up sheets, I couldn't even get close enough to see the events. Whatever they are, looks like a ton of kids want to participate."

"We are doing a few traditional events since kids really look forward to those. The powderpuff game will be on Friday, like always, and we will have a quad-decorating contest where each class will compete against the others. But we are also doing a cool tricycle race and a senior dress-up day where we can all dress up like senior citizens." Talking about spirit week and the senior games is getting me excited about it. I'm finally looking forward to being a part of that week, even if it might not be the way I thought it would be when I ran for this office.

Angie's phone chimes and she reminds Lisa and Mandy they all have a meeting for the school paper that they need to attend. They each give me a hug and then head off to their meeting.

I make my way over to my locker bay and trade out a few things from my locker. I know Rosie was joking when she suggested it, but I do want to go watch Gabe swim. I only have to make it past Brady and Elle and then I can slip into the pool building and be away from the curious eyes of that group. I focus my gaze straight ahead, keeping up a quick pace that silently expresses I'm in a rush. I can see Brady sitting on one of the old wooden benches out of the corner of my eye. A small stab of pain hits my heart when Elle sits down beside him and swings her legs together over his lap. I don't stop to catch my breath or turn to run the other way. Today I just keep putting one foot in front of the other so they don't stop me from getting to where I want to be.

There are a few kids sitting in the bleachers, eating, playing cards, or texting. I sneak up into the back and tuck my backpack at my feet. I watch Gabe as he swims laps, his strokes steady and sure. He reaches the far end of the pool and his coach leans down to tell him something. I study his broad shoulders as he hangs on to the edge, intently listening to the instructions. He nods his head and then climbs out, positioning himself to dive back in.

I admire his dedication to his sport, giving up his lunch hour to practice. Just before the whistle blows, his eyes move up to mine as if he has sensed me there and I see his lips curl slightly. The loud shriek of the whistle snaps him back to the moment and he cuts through the water as if he is but a drop of it himself. I watch him, unable to look away as he pushes forward, focused and determined, until he emerges to talk to the coach again.

I lean back against the bench behind me and watch him as he disappears into the locker room. I only have about ten minutes until my next class, so I decide to stay here and avoid the walk back through the quad. I pull my paperback out of my bag and find my place. I'm lost in the story when I feel him beside me. He moves closer to me and playfully bumps my shoulder with his own. "You're coming tomorrow, right?" he asks.

"Yes. Should I bring anything?" I close my book and turn my head toward him. It's amazing but every time I look at him I am struck anew by how incredible his eyes are.

He moves his foot a little closer to mine, causing his muscular thigh to rest against my leg. In a seemingly innocent move he stretches his arms across the bench behind us and leans back, essentially wrapping his arm around me. "Not a thing. We've got it covered."

The bell rings and the few kids who have been watching practice start filing down the steps. He offers me his hand and pulls me from my seat. Maybe it's because we are late and the halls are empty as we walk to class that I don't worry about running into Brady and Elle, or maybe it's because when I'm with Gabe nothing else seems to matter. I want to spend more time with him. "What are you doing later?" I ask as we stop just outside an empty classroom.

He smiles and shakes his head. "I don't have any plans yet."

"All the talk about prom has made me want to watch *Pretty in Pink*. I was wondering if you'd want to come over and watch it with me." I hope he can't see how anxious I am about inviting him over. I just can't stand the thought of not seeing him again until the barbecue.

"You know I wouldn't pass up an invite like that. What time should I come over?"

"How about seven?"

"Text me your address and I'll see you then." We stand there for a second in the hall as kids push past. It feels like something is changing between us, and I'm not sure how to feel about that. Finally, when the bell rings the last warning to get to class, he takes a step away from me. With a huge grin he says, "Next we can watch *Say Anything*, just to see a guy with a boom box do it right." When my lips curl up he lifts his brows and then turns and heads to his class.

Gabe pulls up at my house just before seven. My parents are out for the evening at the local hospital fund raiser, and I purposely didn't mention inviting Gabe over to Rosie because I want her to keep her plans of going out with Dawn so I can have some time to get to know Gabe. Mom agreed to not mention it, but warned me that they could be home at any time. I laughed and told her it wasn't like that with him, but I could see in her expression that she didn't quite believe me.

I feel nervous suddenly, which is a totally different feeling than I've had with him before. It isn't the typical jittery I feel when I am getting to know someone new. It's more like the anxiety of anticipation. I can't wait to spend time with him. I don't totally understand the feeling—it's not how I was with Brady, but if I'm being honest it isn't how I ever felt with people who were just my friends either. Rosie's advice about how the best way to get over someone is to get under someone else flashes through my head, and I quickly push the thought away. Gabe is just a friend and I'm pretty sure that's all he sees me as too. I hear a knock on the door and practically jump even though I'm expecting it. I take in a big breath and hope he can't see how rattled I am.

"Hey," I say, and step to the side so he can come in.

"Hi." He runs his hand over his head and that small movement gives away that he's a little nervous too.

"Do you like popcorn?" I shut the door and motion for him to follow me into the living room.

"Yeah." He's checking out all the family pictures my mom has hanging on our walls. I leave him by the couch and retrieve the popcorn and two waters. When I get back, he's sitting in the corner of the sofa. I set everything down on the coffee table and grab the remote. I sit down on the other side and get the movie set up. I can feel him watching me as I press the buttons and try to get our old DVD player to cooperate.

After a few minutes of no success, he laughs and scoots

closer to me. "Want me to try?" he asks, holding out his hand for the remote. I hand it to him without a fight.

"Usually that's my dad's job," I explain. He looks over the remote and then taps a few of the buttons. And like magic, the previews begin to play. Only now we're closer than we were before and I can feel his leg pressed up against mine. I wonder if he's going to move away, but he doesn't. He leans back and gets comfy. I follow his lead and do the same.

I'm supposed to be watching what's happening on the screen, but my mind is running a million miles per hour. I *like* him. I knew he was attractive, but over the last few days my interest in him has been changing. I didn't know it until tonight, but now it seems so obvious. I just don't know what to do about it. I don't know if he feels the same way, and even if he does, do I really want to start something when I'm still trying to recover from the last mistake I made?

He turns his head, and I can tell he's surprised to see me looking at him. I quickly turn back to the movie, hoping he will think I've only been looking at him for a second. His arm stretches out across the back of the couch and all I can do is try to relax as his warmth and fresh scent surrounds me. I can't even tell you what's happening in the story because I can't get my thoughts to quiet down. I stare straight ahead, pretending to watch.

Gabe reaches for some popcorn and I feel a piece hit my

cheek. I turn to him and he laughs. "Where are you? Because I know you aren't here watching this movie with me. You look like you're a million miles away in there." He taps my head and tosses a piece of the popcorn into his mouth.

"I'm watching," I protest weakly, and he gives me a knowing smile. He turns his eyes back to the movie and I try to relax again. After a few minutes I finally get into the story. "Are you cold?" I ask when my body temperature cools down. He shakes his head as he looks at me.

"No. Here." He leans forward and pulls his hoodie over his head. He opens the bottom and holds it up so I can tuck my head inside. Every ounce of calm I had managed to project gets thrown out the window when his warmth surrounds me. God, I love this sweatshirt. When I peek out from beneath the hood, our eyes meet. His fingers tug a little on the hood strings. I feel myself moving closer as he pulls me steadily to him. I put my hand on his as he wraps the strings a little tighter, pulling me even closer. His eyes burn into mine. He closes the distance between our lips and I close my eyes as his mouth meets mine. The heat from our contact spreads through me like wildfire, burning up my heart and sending butterflies into flight inside my chest.

His hand releases the strings and slides up to my cheek. His fingers move into my hair and he holds me close. It's amazing and hot, exciting and terrifying, all at the same time. My mind goes fuzzy and my skin heats, my breath racing in and out and mingling with his. He guides me so that I'm flat on my back and he is above me on his side.

His thumb strokes my cheek, sending little flames along my nerves, waking up every part of my body. I finally give into temptation and let my palm lightly brush his face. His skin feels even better than I could have imagined, smooth and then scratchy, strong and yet yielding to my own. I part my lips, inviting his tongue inside, and as it lightly floats across my own, I feel the desire for him building in my stomach and low in my core.

It occurs to me that I might pass out. My heart is pounding and my breathing is rapid, but I ignore my worries and let my fingers run through his hair, loving the way it feels soft in one direction and prickly in the other. He pulls back for a minute to look at my face and I silently beg him to kiss me again. I can already feel the slight bite on my skin where his stubble has scraped against my chin. He rubs his thumb gently across my bottom lip, his chest heaving, and I feel the heat rising off his skin. I thought he was handsome before, but now I want to crawl inside him or, at the very least, kiss every inch of his face and neck.

"Everly," he says on a whisper, and I instantly fall in love with the sound of my name on his lips. "You're always beautiful, but you really should see the way you look right now.

I've wondered what it would be like to kiss you, but it's more incredible than I could have ever guessed."

"Then why did you stop?" I lift my chin a little, bringing my lips slightly closer to his. His eyes are burning with passion, and I run my tongue along my lips, wetting them before pulling my bottom lip between my teeth.

"Now that I can, I'm having trouble taking my eyes off you long enough to do it." I move so that my nose barely brushes next to his as we breathe each other in and out. His eyes close a second before mine, and I think this is what it must feel like to be high when our lips press together again.

His hand moves down to grip my hip and his leg carefully moves over mine until we are tangled together on the couch. In the distance I hear the movie playing, but everything fades into the background when I'm in his arms. I'm not sure when the energy of our friendship shifted into something more, but I know it feels right, even if my experience in this gray area is very limited.

I'm not sure what this means for us, if it means anything. All I know is that I needed this.

seventeen

I HAD A few hours to kill before Gabe's barbecue, so I decided to go to the retirement home. After an hour reading to a few of the women and watching game show reruns with the men, I feel like my old self again. Sitting in my car on Gabe's street, I look down at my phone for the tenth time, checking to make sure I'm at the right address. Finally I climb out, following a few girls up to the front door. They knock and Gabe answers, letting them inside with a hug for each of them. When he turns back around and sees me, my heart jumps a little in my chest as his bright smile stretches across his face. He pulls me into his arms for a brief hug before motioning for me to come inside.

"Come on," he says over his shoulder as he walks through the living room and toward the back of the house. "I want you to meet Maggie." We step outside and the sound of music fills the cooling air. There are about ten girls on the patio, laughing and snacking on chips and veggies. Their eyes follow us as Gabe puts his hand on the small of my back and guides me toward a beautiful redhead curled up in a wooden deck chair.

I immediately see that they share the same eyes. She stands and takes a step toward me. "You must be Everly." She gives me a small hug. "I'm Maggie."

"Nice to meet you," I reply, and it is. She has a warmth about her that puts me at ease. "Thanks for letting me come." Her eyes leave mine to quickly glance at her brother.

"I needed to put a face to the name." It gives me a bit of a buzz, knowing he's been talking to his family about me. "Help yourself to a drink if you'd like and then get my brother going on that grill. We're starving."

Gabe laughs behind me and I turn to see his hands up in surrender. "I'm on it," he says. I grab a soda from the ice chest nearby and then sit down in an empty chair, making sure I've got a good view of him as he puts the hamburgers on the grill. Maggie stands beside him, laughing at something he's said and then poking him in the side as he tries to flip a burger. It's clear how close they are.

The backyard is huge, beautifully landscaped with pavers and green grass. There is a bistro table with two chairs off in one corner and a fire pit surrounded by Adirondack chairs just outside the back sliding doors. I kick off my flip-flops and tuck my feet up underneath me.

"They were still mooing last time," Maggie yells to me with a playful scowl. Gabe rolls his eyes and shuts the lid of the grill.

"Well, maybe I like raw burgers with undercooked potato salad." He puts his arm around her shoulders and pulls her in so he can ruffle her hair. She shrieks and tries to escape, but he is laughing, and by the time he releases her she can barely catch her breath through the giggles.

"You're mean," she scolds, but her smile shows she doesn't mind his teasing. After giving him a playful poke in the ribs she cuts across the grass to head in my direction. The seat beside me is empty so she sits down on it and pulls her cardigan a little tighter as a cool breeze drifts past us. "You know he talks a lot about you," she says, still watching him at the grill.

"All good things, I hope."

Maggie nods and Gabe glances at us, pointing his two fingers at his eyes and then to us as if to say he was watching us. Maggie and I both stick our tongues out at him and then laugh when we realize the other did it too.

"He told me you're a runner," she says, leaning her head back against the chair.

"Not as serious as you. Berkeley is impressive. I don't think I could ever do it competitively."

"Thanks. Maybe we could go together sometime. I didn't think I could run competitively either, but you might be surprised. I have a great soundtrack that helps. It's a blend of a bunch of different types of music. A friend of mine who was a music major told me that listening to songs with a certain number of beats per minute would help me to pace myself." She turns her head toward me and continues, "I could send it to you if you're interested."

"I'd love that! I've been looking for new songs." I take a sip of my drink. "So what are you studying at Berkeley?"

"I was a history major, but I think when I go back I want to switch to psychology. What about you? Have you decided what you're going to do after you graduate?"

"I'm staying local. I was accepted as a liberal arts major at UCLA."

"Well, isn't that convenient?" She sits up in the chair and twists her body so that she's perched on the edge of her seat. "Gabe is going to UCLA too. Swimming for their team in the fall." She shrugs her shoulders and flashes a beautiful smile. A friend calls to her from the other side of the fire. "Don't be a stranger, okay?"

I nod my head and watch as she bounces over to hug a new arrival to the barbecue. I turn back around to look at Gabe. He gestures to me from across the yard to ask if I'm okay. I smile and give him the thumbs-up, my heart thudding in my chest from the news his sister just delivered. For the past few weeks I'd been dreading that I agreed to follow Brady to college. Now I know that I'll at least have a friend there . . . or whatever Gabe is to me now.

I expect to see his parents, but I learn from the scattered conversations that they are out of town until tomorrow morning. When the burgers are ready, Maggie retrieves a platter of buns and a bucket full of condiments from the kitchen. Her friends all jump up and fill their plates, then return to their seats to resume their conversations. It becomes clear to me that this has happened many times before. The girls are all comfortable here as they settle in and talk about anything and everything while they prepare their plates. I feel a little envious that these girls stay in touch and make an effort to get together for Maggie when they most likely work or attend one of the many colleges in the area.

I make my plate and wait as Gabe does the same. We sit with the group and join in their quick conversation. These girls are fast talkers and nothing seems to be off-limits. I hear all about their college adventures, new boyfriends, and dates that went badly. Maggie tells us about her worst date ever and has everyone laughing by the time she's through. "I didn't think that date could get any worse, but then Gabe caught me sneaking in past my curfew and had dirt on me," Maggie says on a sigh.

"You didn't think I'd just let you get away with it, did you? You know you'd have done the same thing in my position." Gabe looks to her with a cocked eyebrow.

"You made me do your laundry for a month, Gabe. That's just cruel." Her whine turns into a big smile when he shrugs his shoulders.

"You made me wash your car after the trip to the desert or you were going to tell Mom that you caught me trying cigarettes with our cousin Joe. Do you have any idea how many bugs I had to scrape off your bumper?"

"Joe's always been trouble," she says, "and that's totally different." We all watch Gabe and Maggie go back and forth playfully, teasing each other about things in their past. What I learn from the exchange is that they never told on each other no matter what they had caught their sibling doing. I also learn that the two of them got into plenty of trouble together as well.

When dinner is finished, Maggie jumps up to grab dessert. Gabe follows her into the kitchen to help. I'm talking to one of her friends about an old teacher that we both had for

English, so I stay where I am and wait for them to come back. After a while I wonder what's taking so long. The teacher conversation is long since over and a few of the girls have started to glance back into the house to see if they can spot them.

When Gabe finally emerges with a tray full of cookies, he sets them down and then grabs a plate and puts a few on it. Maggie sets her tray down as well and moves to sit with a friend close to the back door. I stand up and walk toward the cookies, but Gabe catches my elbow and motions for me to follow him to the secluded seats in the corner. The girls don't pay any attention to us, and we watch the bonfire from a distance as we eat. I'm smiling around a bite of warm, gooey cookie when he speaks low enough for only me to hear. "She's mad at me."

I turn my head toward him and wipe at the spot of chocolate I feel on my lip. "She doesn't seem mad at you."

"She wouldn't want her friends to see." He sets his cookie down and pushes it away like he's lost his appetite. He leans forward and rubs the back of his head, trying to get it together before he speaks again. "I made her take her pill in front of me. Mom and Dad left me responsible and I panicked." He looks over to where his sister is and she catches his eye. I watch her smile fall for the briefest of seconds and imagine the way it must break his heart. A rush of air speeds out of his mouth and his eyes meet mine again.

"What happened?" I whisper.

"She was acting too excited. I thought maybe she hadn't been taking them. It's this fear." He rubs at his chest and leans back in the chair, looking up into the sky. "Those pills are the difference between life and death for her, and my parents left them with me. I begged her to let me see the bottle." He closes his eyes. "She told me it was *her* life. I can't understand how the meds make her feel. She hates them. I just kept saying 'please.'" I reach for the hand still resting on his chest and rub my finger across the back of it.

"You were just doing what you thought was right." I give his hand a squeeze. I know that sharing this with me must be hard. He seems so strong when helping me, but right now I see the cracks in his facade. He's hurting and I just want to be here for him.

"She cried. She put it on her tongue and cried, Everly. She swallowed the pill without water and then opened her mouth wide like they make her do in the hospital, to prove she wasn't cheeking it." He pulls my hand into his. "It hurt. I have to be so many people with her. Sometimes, like right now, I get to be her brother. I say hi to her friends and light the barbecue and we can all laugh and talk. Then other times I have to be on my parents' side against her. I have to tell her what she can and can't do, like she's some little kid."

I push my plate away and move my chair in closer to his. It takes everything I have not to pull him into my arms and comfort him. "If she loves you even half as much as you clearly love her, she'll understand. Sometimes doing what's right feels wrong. What choice do you have? You're trying to keep her healthy. What happened next?"

"She took the bottle and threw it at the wall."

"She took the medication. That's all that matters." I watch his face twist with pain. "Maybe for a while it will feel like an uphill battle, but that doesn't mean you're doing it wrong."

"It's not fair. I'm supposed to be her brother, not her fucking keeper. I force her to take pills that make her miserable so she won't leave us. That's so fucked up." We sit back and watch the girls laughing and then standing and gathering their plates. Maggie makes her way over to us as her friends go inside.

"We're going to the movies. You guys want to come with?" Gabe looks over to me and I shrug my shoulders.

"Thanks, Maggie. I think we're just going to hang out here." He keeps his eyes on hers until she agrees, so many unspoken words passing between them.

"In case you're gone before I get back." She leans over and hugs me again, this time a little tighter and a little longer. "It was nice meeting you."

"You too." Her embrace is different from before, almost defeated. Can she guess what we've been talking about? Is she uncomfortable that I've been let in on their family secret—her secret?

When she turns and walks back toward the house, Gabe slides his phone from his pocket and types out a quick message. He looks up to the group of girls inside the house as if searching for some sort of sign. Finally his phone beeps and he breathes out a sigh of relief. "She has some really amazing friends who have stuck by her through the tough times. The blonde in there"—he sticks his chin in the direction of the house and I see a petite fair-haired girl sliding her purse onto her shoulder—"she told me she'd look after her tonight. I just asked her to text me if anything happens."

When the girls finally leave the living room, Gabe's eyes meet mine. It's so clear to see that some weight has been lifted from his shoulders. His face is more relaxed and I can see a playful smile beginning to emerge. "Having you here made my day a little better. What was the rest of your day like?"

"I volunteered at the retirement home again. It felt good." I squeeze his hand in mine.

"Do you ever get tired of doing everything right?" He smiles when he says it, but I can tell he is being serious.

"Not until recently. I used to live for being perfect for

everyone. I've surprised myself lately by how much I've let my mood get in the way of following the rules. This year I ditched class for the first time and flat-out didn't show up to a few of my regular commitments. What about you? What kind of bad side are you hiding?"

"You'd blush if I told you." His eyes stare right into mine and I feel heat climb up my neck to my cheeks. Last night he kissed me until we heard my parents pull into the drive-way. We both fled to opposite ends of the couch and tried not to laugh while we waited for them to open the door. It didn't give us any time to talk about what had happened, but I thought a lot about it after he left. I liked that the kiss and the excitement of being with him had chased away my heart-ache for a while. I'm not ready to dive into anything serious, but maybe Dawn and Rosie have the right idea.

I cock my head to the side and say, "Try me."

"You wouldn't be saying that if you could see what I was thinking." His crooked smile tips me over the edge and makes me feel drunk with lust. I notice my breathing change. His free hand moves lightly to my neck, his thumb slowly sliding over my pulse there.

"Why don't you show me then." I don't even know who I am anymore. I've never been this bold, but I've also never wanted to get lost in someone as much as I do with Gabe. This time it's his breath that catches and his mouth is on mine, hot and needy. He kisses me greedily and I love it. I feel wanted and desired, something special that he can't get close enough to.

He pulls away after a few minutes; our chests are heaving and our hearts are racing. My face is flushed and my lips are swollen from his kisses. He stands and offers me his hand. I feel nervous, unsure of what will happen, but I put my hand in his and let him pull me to my feet. His arms circle my waist and I wrap my arms around his neck. Until now, he's been the one always holding me. This time I hold him, pulling him to me and standing firm. The night is dark around us, the flames from the fire are gone, and only a slight red glow from the embers remains.

His lips feather against the sensitive skin below my ear and along my neck. I close my eyes and fill my lungs with his scent as I hold him close. "Come inside with me."

"Yes," I say and I pull back, holding his face in my hands. This time I move first, pressing my lips to his, loving the way he responds. He lightly sucks my bottom lip into his mouth before stepping back, grabbing my hands, and pulling me into the house. I can't believe I'm about to take my sister's crazy cheer practice advice. Friend, boyfriend, or our own place in between, it doesn't matter right now. I just want to feel good and I know we can do that for each other.

As I cross the threshold of Gabe's bedroom my confidence begins to waver a little. I can't seem to quiet the worried voice in my head, and a wave of fear rushes over me as I question how capable I am of living up to what he's imagined all this time. My heart flutters in my chest and I steady my breathing, concentrating on four slow counts in and four slow counts out.

I get the feeling that Gabe is picking up on my growing anxiety as he unhurriedly moves toward me, reaching for my waist. I watch his hand getting closer and with a small glance I can see his eyes watching to make sure this is what I want. And deep down I know that I do. I want to feel good again even if it isn't going to last forever. My hip seems to move on its own accord, turning to meet his palm.

I feel it the moment he touches me, the tingle that begins where his warm hand rests just above my hip, then gradually climbs up my body. His gaze pierces mine as he tugs me closer and his muscles flex as he presses himself against me. His free hand brushes the side of my neck and his fingers tangle into my hair, tipping my face up to his. I breathe him in and thoughts of anything but the way his lips will press against mine flee from my mind.

My body ignites with a steady hum of heat and pulse when his thumb slips beneath the hem of my shirt and caresses the skin underneath. I close my eyes as an intense sensation starts to build within me, insistently aching to be released. As if perfectly in tune with the inner workings of my body, Gabe slides his hand a little lower on my hip, splays it out, and then pulls me to him, pressing his body tighter against mine.

His face is so close, his nose brushing against my cheek as he closes the remaining distance between our lips. His fingers in my hair grow more urgent, tightening their hold and bringing me so close we seem to blend together. Our tongues slide along each other, retreating only to plunge back in. I tuck my hands beneath his T-shirt on each side, needing to feel his skin. I let my palms roam up his tensed back, loving the feel of his muscles contracting beneath them. He pulls his hands away from me to reach over his head and remove his shirt. My teeth dig into my bottom lip as I take in the broad, tan chest in front of me.

After giving me a moment to explore his chest with my eyes, he hooks his fingers under the hem of my shirt and looks at me for approval. I nod my head and raise my arms, feeling another surge of excitement as he slides the fabric up and off my body. I stand before him in only my pink bra, the small satin bow buried between my breasts.

"You're more beautiful than I imagined." His voice is rough and deep, drawing me in and making me drunk with excitement. He moves his hands to my sides and presses against me again, tucking his face into the curve of my neck. I love the faint scratch of his cheek as he runs his face up to my ear, sucking it gently. My knees begin to buckle, but he holds onto me tightly, continuing his exquisite torture— tongue and teeth, smooth and rough—along my neck.

My arms are resting on his shoulders, and I lean my head back, urging him to kiss down the other side of my neck too. His tongue licks softly along my collarbone before slipping lower. Finally his hand caresses me and never in my life have I felt so lit up with raw need.

Of course, that is the exact moment that his phone begins to ring. It takes us a minute to shake the fog from our heads and separate so he can answer the call. It feels like I'm floating, every nerve in my body pulsing and afire. I close my eyes, fanning my face to relieve the heat flushing my cheeks. I scramble for my shirt, suddenly worried we're moving so fast. Once I've pulled it over my head, I turn around and watch him. His back is to me and he has his phone to his ear, the other hand rubbing worriedly through his hair.

"She went out with her friends." I hear only his side of the conversation. "Yes, she took her pill . . . okay, I'll see you guys soon." His shoulders slump as he disconnects. He turns to me and tosses the phone on the bed. "My parents are on their way back. They're worried about us. Maggie called them earlier and told them that we'd gotten into a disagreement." He looks down to the floor.

"I should go. They've never met me and I don't think it would look too good if they found us here alone together." I smile at him reassuringly when he looks up and nods in agreement.

He retrieves his shirt from the ground and pulls it back on, covering his chest. "I don't want you to go, but you're probably right." He moves to stand in front of me, chastely kissing my lips while entwining his fingers with mine at our sides. "I'm really glad you came tonight, Everly."

I roll up onto my toes and press another kiss to his lips. "Thanks for inviting me. I had a lot of fun." I feel my cheeks flush again and he smiles, squeezing my hand in his. He leads me down the hall and to the front door. Before reaching for the knob, he turns to face me. His hands touch my face softly as he kisses me goodnight. I feel no regret as I leave his house, but a part of me wonders if it will surface as soon as I'm alone in my room.

eighteen

IT FEELS GREAT to wake up on my own instead of to the sound of an alarm insisting I get up. I peek at my clock and see that it is only eight in the morning. My family never expects me to be up so early on Sundays—even when I do wake up, I usually cover my head and stay in bed until someone comes to pull me out. Today though I feel like taking advantage of the beautiful weather.

After a trip to the bathroom I get dressed in my running clothes and dig my shoes out from under a pile in my closet. I love running, but I haven't been out for a while. It's hard to think about exercise when you are struggling even to eat.

I've been doing better with that too, and I feel a little proud as I tie my laces. I can hear my parents' TV and smell the rich scent of coffee, so I don't bother to grab my front door key, but I tuck my phone into my bra after starting up my music and putting in my earbuds.

As my feet hit the pavement I quickly fall back into my rhythmic breathing. The sound of a guitar in my ears makes me smile. I downloaded Ed Sheeran's albums as soon as I got home the night I watched the planes with Gabe. The songs help me to pace myself as I run along the sidewalk and up and down the small hills in my neighborhood. I feel the sweat beading and dripping down my back and head. I'm not a fast runner, but I've worked my way up to four miles at a time and love getting lost in the rhythm of it.

I alter my usual path since it would bring me right down Brady's street, but I can't help but glance in the direction of his house as I run along the street perpendicular to his. In the distance I see his car in the driveway and then my eyes land on Elle's car, parked across the street. I feel my feet falter below me and I force myself to keep going up the next block.

Stopping because the burning lump in my throat is making it too hard to breathe, I rest my hands on my knees and try to suck in air. I shouldn't care anymore. Hasn't it been enough time? I give myself a minute to rein it all in and then start running again, faster this time, until I'm in a full sprint as I fly up my driveway.

My parents are still in their room when I make my way down the hallway. Rosie's door is shut. I close my bedroom door behind me and pull the latest log out of my book, unfolding and straightening it on my desk. The first pen I grab is out of ink, but the second one works and I quickly write down my thoughts.

Situation: She stayed over at his house.
Feelings: OUCH. Panic, fear, hurt. Stomachache, sharp
   chest pain.
Unhelpful Thoughts: He loves her more than me. She is
   already a part of his family. I've been replaced.
Alternative Thoughts: He will hurt her eventually too. I
   only saw her car because I was out getting on with
   my life.

I toss the pen and fold my arms on the desk, resting my head on top of them. I close my eyes and try to focus only on the alternative thoughts. I don't feel like I've come far enough in getting on with my life. I want to so badly, but I can't push the hurt from my heart. I pull my phone from my bra and shut down the music that has been lost in the background of my crazy thoughts. I let my fingers linger over the keys. It might not be right to share my feelings about this with Gabe, but I can talk to him about something else so that I won't feel so alone. I pull up his contact so I can begin my text to him, but a bubble pops up on the screen letting me know that Gabe is writing a text to me. I smile, so grateful to have him right now.

GABE: What are you doing two Tuesdays from now, after counseling? I just bought two tickets to a concert you have to see. Would your parents let you out late?

ME: Please tell me it's Ed Sheeran!

GABE: Does that mean you'll go with me?

ME: Yes! My parents won't care. They sort of loosened the reins when I turned eighteen.

GABE: I'll pick you up next Tuesday morning before school. We'll go to our appointment together and leave from there.

I sit staring at my phone with a big smile on my face. I grab my pen and write a quick note at the bottom of my log when a new alternative thought enters my mind.

I survived another big moment. Soon there will be no more of these moments left to survive and I'll be able to start living my life without fear of being hurt by them anymore.

After my shower I sit in the living room with my parents, watching a recorded reality show they like, waiting for the right time to bring up my plans for next Tuesday night. I'm pretty sure it won't be an issue, but I don't know if I'm ready to answer the questions they might have about my relationship with Gabe. My mom reaches for my hand beside her on the couch.

"You went running today?" she asks with a smile, and my dad leans forward so he can see my face when I answer.

"Yeah. It felt good. I'm trying to start doing the things I used to." I smile at them and hope they get a small reprieve from their parental worry.

"That's great. You should get out more," my dad says before taking a sip of his coffee.

"So would it be okay if I went to a concert next Tuesday night, then?" My mom looks to my dad and he gives her a nod.

"What concert and who are you going with?" my mom asks, resting her mug in her lap.

"Ed Sheeran. Gabe asked me to go." I don't miss the way my mom's eyes widen with surprise and my dad's features twitch a little at the mention of the boy he'd only met quickly just a few days ago.

"Will he be driving you or are you taking your car?" my dad asks.

"He's actually going to pick me up before school next Tuesday, then we're going to leave after my appointment."

"I think that's wonderful. I'll give you some money for gas and dinner." My mom turns her attention back to the TV, but pats my hand reassuringly.

"Thanks." I get up and head down the hall, deciding to ask Rosie to make a trip to the mall with me for a new outfit after I take the girls around to a few garage sales. It shouldn't be hard to convince her since she practically lives there when she isn't at practice.

With the day planned, I pick the girls up and head to Starbucks so we can drink fancy coffees while we drive around the neighborhood looking for the lawns covered in items that might help decorate the quad with our theme. We find old beach balls, worn beach chairs, and even a surfboard that will look great propped up in the sand. I was able to find a few good deals on Craigslist, so we pick up those items as well. We stop for a late breakfast at McDonald's before stashing our items away in the back of Angie's garage. Kathy has promised us the sand is sitting safely on her father's lot. I can feel the excitement for the prank building inside me, and I love the feeling. It reminds me of what I thought the end of my senior year would be like before my heartbreak.

Rosie and I get to the mall just after lunch and shop until it's almost dinnertime. We laugh and try on a million things just for the fun of it. When we sit down for dinner at a restaurant on the outside of the mall, I decide it's time to fill her in on Gabe.

"So do you think you like him?" she asks as soon as the waitress leaves our table.

"I like spending time with him," I hedge. "And our kisses were incredible." Rosie laughs at what I can only imagine is the dreamy expression on my face. "But honestly, I'm not prepared to dive back into the deep end of the dating pool. Everything that happened with Brady and Elle is still so raw and I just don't think I'm ready to get into something serious with everything else. It's hard though, because when I'm with Gabe I'm happy—really happy—but when I'm not with him I sometimes catch myself thinking about Brady." I watch my sister think about what I've said. She takes a sip of her soda when the waitress comes back to take our order, then she leans in as if to share a secret.

"Then you need to spend more time with Gabe. Hang out with him until there is more of him than Brady. I mean, would you even want Brady back after all he's put you through?" She isn't being mean, just asking the same honest question I've asked myself over and over again.

I sigh. "It isn't really Brady in my heart, it's his ghost. It's the person I thought he was. I see traces of the Brady I love, but then he does something that makes me wonder who he is now. I think all the parts of him I love are living inside me. I think it has stopped being about him and is now just me holding on to our history."

She thinks for a minute and then smiles over her drink. "We need someone to exorcise him from your heart. I don't think we could get a priest, but I happen to know a really hot swimmer who might just be the man for the job." I almost spit out my drink when I start laughing.

"Maybe."

"Well, you are going on a date with him. Doesn't that mean something?"

"I wouldn't call it a date. I mean, I know we kissed, but neither of us have made a move to make it anything serious, and I'm not sure that's a bad thing. I enjoy our friendship and don't want to risk losing that. He's my first new friend since losing Brady and Elle. I'm afraid if we move things into a relationship, it might fall apart. I don't think I can survive another heartbreak like that right now."

"You don't know that will happen," she says, taking a sip from her straw and then shaking her head. "He's different. The situation is different. YOU are different."

She's right, but still I can't help but think that I thought Brady was different too. I would hear about the longer relationships at our school breaking up during their senior year and believed that would never happen to us. I believed that we were different. "I don't trust myself to see the signs."

"Don't give it a label then. Don't call it a 'relationship' if that word freaks you out. Just go out with him as friends who are really into each other. Do what feels right at the time without overthinking everything. Just give it a chance to become more if that's what you both decide that you want." The waitress returns with our pizza.

"You make it sound easy."

"You don't have to make it complicated," she counters. I laugh as I steal a pepperoni off her piece and shove it into my mouth before she can do anything about it.

Her eyes meet mine across the table. "It's good to have you back, Everly. I really missed you." She offers me a smile and I nod my head, realizing I haven't been the only one to have lost someone these last few weeks.

nineteen

DRIVING INTO THE nearly empty parking lot on Monday morning feels surreal. It's only six thirty a.m. as I park my car and nudge Rosie awake in the passenger seat. She opens her eyes slowly, struggling to focus through the thick fog that is lurking in the parking lot and giving the school an eerie vibe. "You still have pillow lines on your cheek." I laugh as I flip down her visor and open the small vanity mirror. She makes a face as she runs her fingers across the angry red indents.

"Why do we have to be here so early?" she asks again. We've already been over this, but every time she falls back to sleep she seems to forget . . . or maybe she just asks a million times as a form of revenge for me dragging her here just minutes after the sun has come up.

"It's spirit week," I deadpan. I reach behind us and pull one of her crunchy pom-poms from the back and drop it unceremoniously into her lap. The glittery plastic strands make even this time of the morning feel festive. "You know, the week where cheerleaders are supposed to be cheery." My sarcasm is on point even though my brain has only been awake an hour.

"I can be cheery at eight a.m. I don't need to be cheery right now." She rolls her eyes playfully and then points out the window at the plants that decorate the front planters. "See, nothing is awake right now." I chuckle when I see the usually tall flowers hanging limply, covered in morning dew. Angie's car pulls into the spot next to us, blocking our view of the sleepy blooms. She's smiling and waving to us, and I have to give Rosie credit when she finds the energy to smile and shake a pom-pom in her direction. "You owe me," she says as she unbuckles her seat belt.

I love being at school this time of the morning. The moisture and fog rolling in from the ocean turn our usually boring old school buildings into mysterious structures. They act as a filter, turning decades of wear into preserved historical landmarks full of mystery. When the sun burns it all away second period, the sights before me will turn back into the chipped and weathered classrooms. I tug Rosie along as Angie joins us and we head to the student council office.

"Good morning, ladies," Mrs. Cramier says when we step inside. The heater has kicked on even though later we will all be wishing for AC instead.

"Good morning," we say together. After setting our bags down we open the storage room and grab as many of the posters as we can. More students make their way into the room, some of them chipper and excited for the week, and others groggy and nursing large coffees. We hand them the posters and direct them to where we want them hung. Then together we start pulling out the balloons and filling them with helium from the ancient-looking metal tanks.

"Where did you even learn how to make these?" Rosie asks as Angie and I take turns blowing up the colorful balloons, tying them, twisting three together, and sliding the group onto a ribbon. We are building a balloon arch that will float over the school entrance and notify students there is something special planned today.

I shrug my shoulders and pull on the knot. "It's something that student council people pass down to each other. A tradition, I guess." Angie nods her head in agreement. "We make at least ten a school year. I think I could do this in my sleep."

"It's cool," Rosie says softly, reaching for a balloon and joining the assembly line.

"Did you remember your pass?" I ask Angie.

"Yes. I will meet you here fourth period to help you get the track set up. We aren't really working on anything important in class so it won't be an issue." The senior games start today and our first activity is the tricycle race. With the senior games and spirit week combined, as has been the tradition for the last ten years, this will be a crazy week for Angie and me. We have to run all the activities, which means we have to manage our fellow council members and make sure everyone has a signed pass for any time they will be missing their classes to help us set up. I feel my lips curl up in a smile. I'm enjoying this. Even with the anxiety and pressure, this is going to be a great week.

"I updated our senior class Facebook page last night. We have everything we need for tomorrow. I think we actually have more than we need. If everyone gets out of bed and to our quad by seven a.m, we should be able to pull it off." I grab another balloon and stretch it out so it's easier to fill.

Rosie slides on another layer. "We are totally going to kick your ass," she says just loud enough so Mrs. Cramier can't hear. "Red is bright and it is going to be everywhere." Class colors are used to promote class spirit. Rosie's class is red, and the senior class is blue. Next year, our color will be passed on to incoming freshmen. Tomorrow is the quad-decorating competition. Each class has chosen a theme around their color and will try to win by impressing the teachers who have volunteered to judge. The winning class gets bragging rights, and will get the most desired seating area at the rally on Friday.

Angie and I exchange a look over the helium tank as Rosie stretches her balloon. She and I have organized the entire thing for our class, and from what we hear, the other classes are far less organized. "Speaking of red," Angie says, "did you remember to tell the staff that they are to wear red for the staff versus seniors basketball game on Wednesday?"

"Yes. I sent out a reminder email on Saturday. I'll send another on Tuesday. Did you talk to Coach about using the football field for practice at lunch?" The sign-ups for the powderpuff game were a huge success. We have enough girls for two teams. The boys who were asked to coach us will be perfect. I wonder if Brady is disappointed he wasn't asked. Today is the first day we will all meet to choose teams and start practicing. It's not a lot of time, but we will meet at lunch this week to practice and stay after school for a two-hour session before the Friday game.

"Yeah. He said we are all set. He just wants us to remind the girls that the turf can give you a nice burn, so we might want to protect our knees and elbows." Angie slides a few balloons on as John, the freshman class president, peeks his head in.

"We're all finished putting up the posters. Do you need any more help to set up before lunch?" A few other kids gather behind him.

"No, I think we have it. Just make sure you're there to help cheer the seniors on."

"You got it," he says, smiling, as he leaves us.

The three of us focus on the arch, the loud sound of the helium tank, and the unnerving sound of skin manipulating latex filling the room. After a few more layers Angie meets my gaze. "I talked to Ethan about the teams," she says cautiously. I feel my heart pick up its pace in my chest. I have been trying to think of what I'd do if Elle and I were chosen for the same team, and I just can't come up with anything that wouldn't add more drama.

She ties her balloon. "I told him it would be awesome if there wasn't any conflict on the teams. I reminded him that Jennifer and Rachel don't get along, and that there might be a few other girls who would prefer to be separated."

"I'll live," I tell her, because it's true. It might be hard to be on a team with Elle, but I am determined to not let her ruin this too.

"Of course," she says quickly. "But he assured me that he and Hector would keep that in mind when they chose teams this afternoon." I feel relieved and let out a big breath of air. "He also told me to tell you he said hi and that he's going to try to get you on his team." She smiles coyly. I feel my cheeks flush. Angie and Rosie both laugh.

"Thank you."

"You're welcome," she replies. We work a little longer and then Rosie leaves so she can chat with her friends before her first class. Angie and I keep working, hoping to get the arch done quickly so we can get it up before most students get on campus. Before long, she and I are the only people left and she whispers, "I can't wait for Sunday night." Her eyes are practically twinkling with excitement.

"Me either."

twenty

I LIE ON my bed feeling more excited than I've been in a long time. My heart is racing and my hands are a bit shaky as I wait in the darkness for the sound of Gabe's truck. It's going to be hard carrying all the props for the prank with my sore arms. I lift my arm and feel the muscle pull tight, the evidence of a week spent working hard learning how to catch and throw a football. I can't help but feel proud of how well my team worked together, and if I close my eyes, I can still imagine the feeling of sweet victory as we scored the last touchdown.

This past week has been one of the craziest of my life.

I've been up each morning before the sun to get to school and prepare for the day's activities, and then I've spent every lunch practicing with my team only to practice again for at least another hour after school. I even had to cancel my therapy appointment Tuesday so I could practice with the girls and still have time after to set up the gym for the staff versus seniors basketball game on Wednesday. I'm exhausted, but very satisfied with the huge success of spirit week.

The seniors won the quad-decorating competition, but the freshmen showed everyone that they are a force to be reckoned with. Angie and I walked over to the freshman quad while the teachers were judging, and both of us were surprised at how the kids pulled together to create an amazing jungle scene. I saw the way they studied the other teams and how they seemed to be taking note of what worked and how to improve. If I had to bet money, I'd say next year that class will sweep the competition. Our underwater theme was creative, but only a small group of us know just how brilliant it was given that we are using a lot of the props again tonight to carry out the senior prank.

I hear the rumbling of an engine and my insides, which were jittery before, are now rolling and bouncing with the excitement of spending time with Gabe. I've barely seen him at all this week, with the exception being during our Thursday Seriously Seniors costume contest. I was the emcee of the event, but Gabe stole the show with his over-the-top costume. I sneak another look at the picture of us I've saved as the background on my phone before tucking it into my pocket and heading downstairs.

I close the door quietly when I climb into his truck. My parents know where I'm going, but I still don't want to wake the entire neighborhood. The second I see Gabe's smiling face I realize how much I've missed him this week. My heart wobbles a little at the sight of him. "Hey, stranger," he says as I buckle my belt.

"Hey," I answer. "Sorry I've been so busy." He pulls out of the driveway and we head to Kathy's father's work yard, where we will be picking up the sand. There should be four other trucks there to do the same.

"You kicked ass this week. Everyone is still talking about how fun it was."

"Thanks."

"And everyone now knows that you are one hell of a lineman." His words make my cheeks lift higher. I'm trying hard not to smile like a lunatic. "I'm not kidding," he says, nudging me a little with his elbow. "You put Teresa on her ass."

"I feel so bad about that. I didn't mean to knock her over, but she was being super aggressive."

"Yeah, her team got a little desperate there at the end."

It's unspoken between us that Elle's team was trampled by mine. I thought it would be really important to me that I beat her, but once I got out there on the bright-green turf with my teammates and new friends, I had a blast and didn't really care if we won or not.

"I'm just glad prom isn't this weekend. I'm sure some of those turf burns and bruises are going to take a while to heal. It will be funny to see how many girls show up in pretty dresses and healing wounds."

"Were you surprised Elle made top ten for prom queen?" he asks me delicately, knowing that I had to hand the sash over to her at the rally.

"No. I always knew she'd make the court at least. I bet she'll be announced queen on prom night. Only in fairy tales does the villain get what's coming to her." He nods at my words, and I let that train of thought play out in my head. When I saw her name it made my heart sink. It was the first time in weeks I had to look her in the eye and, to be honest, that was hard. She didn't say anything to me as I hung her sash, but I could feel her eyes on mine the whole time. "I actually feel a little sad about the whole thing."

"What do you mean?" We pull up in front of the address Angie gave me, and Gabe cuts the engine after parking behind Teresa's lifted truck.

"All the other girls couldn't keep their eyes off the sash

as I put it on them. They were giddy and squealing, so it was hard to put it over their heads. But when I put Elle's on she watched me instead. It was like that sash weighed a million pounds and I was resting it all on her shoulders. I think it might have hurt her to get it from me." I pull the handle and open my door, causing the light to turn on and fill the cab.

"She did a terrible thing to you. Sometimes what we think is going to taste so sweet turns rotten when it's soaked in all the nastiness of what we did to get it." He pulls the keys from the ignition and opens his door. Before we join the other seniors outside in the dark he turns back to me. "I saw the way Brady looked at you when you hung his sash." Just that small reminder makes my stomach turn sour.

I'd seen the way my hands were shaking as I lifted the sash over Brady's head. He'd watched me too, and it felt like he was hoping for forgiveness instead of a silly scrap of fabric. I only had a second before I had to announce the next name, and I struggled to find something to say to him while the microphone wasn't by my lips. In the end, all I could do was shrug my shoulders. Our student body might not have been able to see that he didn't deserve their admiration, but I knew.

"Everly!" My name is called, pulling my attention away from Gabe. I can hear Angie's voice and see the beam of a flashlight being bounced around. "Get over here!" Gabe comes around to my side and hands me a heavy flashlight. We make our way over to the huge pile of sand.

"This is going to be awesome," I can't help but say when a large bulldozer scoops up some sand and takes it to the back of another truck. Kathy is a bit of a spitfire, but watching her drive her father's bulldozer with her safety goggles and a look of determination makes me proud that she's my friend. It takes less than an hour to fill the truck beds with the sand and then we are on our way to the high school. A few seniors are already putting up the props we saved from the quad-decorating contest, the great finds we picked up last Sunday morning at the garage sales, and the items we're borrowing from the drama classroom. By the time we drive Gabe's truck across the basketball courts at the back of the school, it's almost two a.m. It took us over two hours to load the sand and gather the items from Angie's house. We also stopped by two more houses on the way, where seniors had helped by putting out beach items on the curb for students with trucks to bring over to the school.

The trucks have all turned off their lights and backed up to the lunch tables just outside the quad. Kids start spilling out from the other cars parked in the dark and another group that's already begun setting up emerges from the hallway. I feel a little teary as I look around at all the kids under the glow of flashlights. Kids who have never spoken to each other before are working together. It doesn't seem to matter who's popular and who's not, all the groups blend together to become one group of seniors. Drama kids are passing buckets of sand to the jocks, and the metal heads are helping the band students stabilize the wooden palm tree. Elle and Brady are here too, but they respect the distance I try to keep between us, and help on the fringes of the quad as I direct students from the center. I wish every day of high school could have been like this. There is a hopeful part of me that wonders if maybe we've all grown up and we'll leave this school on the same playing field again—throwing all the labels away.

Gabe and I get to work, and two hours later sixty seniors huddle together on the beautiful beach we've made to take a picture. The lighting is terrible and our figures are grainy, but some of the best moments just can't be captured in still frame. I'm smiling when Gabe drops me off at my house, his hoodie keeping me warm, my shoes hanging from my finger because I couldn't resist stepping into one of the small pools filled with water. In a few hours the rest of the student body is going to walk onto campus and find themselves knee-deep in sand under the shade of a giant wooden palm tree. Maybe they won't remember everything they learned in chemistry, or the combination to their lockers, but years from now they will remember the day they sat on the beach in the middle of quad four.

twenty-one

I'M SURE THERE have been pranks far more epic than the one we pulled off, but yesterday morning as the students spilled onto campus and found themselves on a beach, I realized this year's prank will become a legend. I'm still finding sand in my shoes. It took two hours for the teachers on the bottom floor to move away enough of the beach to open their classrooms, and while that might seem like a crime punishable to the highest degree, I think the staff appreciated that nothing was permanent and no real damage was done. We can thank last year's seniors for gluing all the locks shut and providing the staff this year with a little perspective. It could have been worse. Instead, all the seniors crammed into quad four to eat their lunches on the white sand and enjoy a day at our faux beach party.

The day of the concert I've set my alarm to go off thirty minutes earlier than usual so I'll have time to style my hair before school. After my shower I make sure to wear the lotion I was wearing the day I met Gabe, a sweet fruity scent with a small amount of glitter in it. Just enough to make my skin look like it's got a glow.

I blow-dry my hair and then curl it in wide curls down my back. I put my makeup on with the knowledge it will have to last me all day and into the night. My outfit for today is quite a change from what I typically wear to school, but I want something special for tonight. The tight black jersey skirt and formfitting white shirt with cap sleeves look feminine as they hug the lines of my body and show off all my best assets. I slip on a pair of Toms, not wanting my feet to be too sore by the end of the day.

Rosie's face lights up when I run into her in the hallway. "You look so pretty, Everly!" She pulls me into a hug, careful not to squish any of my long curls.

"Thank you. Wish me luck." I straighten up and head for the kitchen for a bowl of cereal before rushing back into our tiny bathroom to brush my teeth. I look at myself in the mirror and feel like I've been hiding this whole time, only to emerge a brighter person today.

I hear the rumble of Gabe's engine when he pulls up outside and I grab my bag and swing it over my shoulder. My mom gives me a wave from the kitchen as I open the front door and make my way to Gabe. He's already out of the truck and on his way toward the house when he stops dead in his tracks. He takes me in from my feet to the top of my head in a slow gaze that has my blood heating up. When his eyes finally meet mine I see the interest in them.

"Wow," he says in a way that I'm not sure I was meant to hear.

He opens the door for me and I climb in. He smiles before going around to the driver's side and then again when he settles in behind the wheel. He laughs a little and I feel my brows pull together, thinking maybe I misread the heat in his eyes a moment ago. "Everly, you look so good I don't know if I'm going to be able to look away from you long enough to get us to school safely."

"Thank you," I say, and feel my own smile growing even though I try to contain it. My cheeks feel warm as he nods his head and then pulls us out onto the road. I watch him drive, carefully taking in his features and noticing the way his eyes look tired and lost. "How are things going with your sister?"

"She's doing okay, I guess. My parents keep insisting that they didn't come home early from their trip because of our fight, but they aren't very good at lying." He shrugs his shoulders and adjusts his arms so that one is resting on the door and the other is draped over the steering wheel.

"How are you doing?" I would swear I can see a million thoughts floating across his face before he finally responds.

"I'm doing okay, too. I told my parents I can't be the one asking her to take her medicine when they're gone. It's making me hate the one thing that gives us any hope for control and peace. I hate those pills." His eyes find mine. "I won't let those pills destroy my relationship with her."

"I get it. I wouldn't want anything like that to come between Rosie and me. Someone should be looking out for what's right for Maggie, but I think telling your parents that it's not going to be you is what's best for you and your sister."

We fall silent as we wait at the last light before turning into the school parking lot. When we pull into the school I feel a little nervous to walk in looking so different. Gabe comes around and opens the door for me, not scooting back as I slide down from the high seat. His eyes pierce mine before dropping to my lips. I feel my tongue slip out to wet them as he leans close to me, passing my lips to whisper in my ear.

"You're killing me in this outfit." He reaches past me to grab my bag and holds it out for me. I take it and we walk through the main gate, my heart still racing from the look in his eyes. The second we clear the hallway together my eyes meet Brady's. The look on his face makes my heart jump with recognition. It takes a split second to remember that I'm not doing this for his attention. His eyes dip down to take in the whole picture before looking back at my face. I notice my pace has slowed a little when Gabe's hand softly touches my back, guiding me over to my locker. I don't know if Gabe noticed him looking, and I don't even care. Brady looking at me doesn't feel right like it used to, and I'm happy to be in the company of someone who sees me the way Gabe does.

"I'll see you at lunch." Gabe smiles at me. The bell rings and he takes a few backward steps before exiting the locker bay.

I should have listened to Laura weeks ago when she told me to "Fake it till you make it," and encouraged me to dress the way I wanted to feel. Now I understand the message she was trying to give me. I feel lighter and happier. Today it seems like everyone is looking my way. More of my old friends approach me throughout the morning and I wonder if it's because I have a smile on my face again.

Even with all the attention, the only person I truly want to spend time with is Gabe. When I find him at my locker at the beginning of lunch, I almost want to kiss him right there. He tries to hide his smile as I make my way across the quad to where he is waiting, but I can see the twitch of his lips right before he loses the battle and a full smile spreads across his face. He's shaking his head when I reach him.

"If I have to hear about how hot you look from one more guy today I might have to start breaking noses."

"Shut up," I tease, giving him a small punch in the arm. I find my lunch bag and we walk over to what I've begun to think of as our place. Today the energy between us feels charged. I fight the urge to touch him and can't help but let my gaze linger on him a little longer than before. When there are only a few minutes left of the period, he scoots closer to me on the bench so that our legs are pressed together. His hand slips around to my lower back. It feels wonderful to be this close to him even if there is a chance that other kids will see.

When the bell rings, his eyes fall to my lips. I'm so tempted to kiss him, even just to stroke his face or run my hands through his hair, but doing so in front of our class-mates might force us to define our relationship . . . and I'm not ready to do that yet.

The rest of the day seems to drag on and I don't feel free until I'm taking my place on the bleachers, waiting for Gabe to be released from practice. He notices me the second I walk in, swimming over to my side of the pool and splashing a little water out at me. The coach calls him back when the other guys finish their laps and I wait for him to take a quick shower before we leave for counseling.

It feels weird yet oddly comfortable to drive to Laura's with him. He reaches across the bench seat and takes my hand in his, holding it the entire ride. I tell him about the kid who tipped over his desk and was trapped for a while in my fifth period class. As the two of us drive along, I almost ask him if we're still just friends. I haven't started a relationship in so long I forget how it all goes. I'm still contemplating all of it when we enter the waiting room and take our seats on the low couch. Our friend is in her usual seat, her jaw dropping to the floor when we walk in together and he rests his arm behind me on the couch.

His therapist gets him first, and I glance at the clock to see if Laura is running late. Finally, after a few more minutes, her door opens, and as her previous client leaves she motions for me to come in. I'm holding only my thought log, having left everything else in Gabe's truck. She squints her eyes at me and then kicks her feet up onto the edge of the ottoman. "You look great. Is this the girl you were before Brady or the one you want to become?"

"The one I want to become." I'd been thinking about it all day. It feels good to take care of myself. She nods her approval and I feel happy with that.

"So what's been going on, Everly?"

"Time," I answer teasingly.

"That it has, that it has." She rocks back in her seat and gestures to the folded paper on my lap.

I unfold the thought log and hand it to her. "I think I'm getting better at this," I say as she stands and makes a copy for her records. "It helps a little more now." She hands it back to me and reviews the copy she's holding.

"I'm glad it's working for you. Do you have any questions about it?" She spins her pen in her hand.

"No, not about that."

"Oh, about other things?" She stops spinning her pen and waits for me to continue.

"When will I know if it's okay to start a new relationship? If I do it too soon will it fall apart?" I grab a pillow and hold it to me.

"There isn't a magic equation for that. You just have to go with your gut. If it feels good to be with the new person and if you can give him a fair shot at building something without thoughts of Brady flooding your head when you're together, then you're ready."

"How do I know if I can give him a fair shot?" I kick my shoes off and tuck my feet underneath me.

"Only your heart can guide you. Are you thinking of seeing someone?" Her question makes my cheeks heat a bit.

"I think I might be already. He knows about my history with Brady and he seems to understand that I sometimes have a hard time separating my life now from my life before."

Laura nods her head. "What is life like now?"

I begin to pull at a long string on the pillow. "I've built stronger friendships outside of Elle and Brady. At lunch I've been sitting with other friends when I'm not committed to a peer mediation shift. There are a few really important new people in my life, but this time it doesn't feel like my whole world is revolving around someone else."

She writes something down and then looks back up to me. "You're afraid all of that will stop again if things don't work out with someone new?" I let go of the string and look up into her eyes. She leans in, hugging her knees a little to close some distance.

"It was just so hard to find the energy to get back into everything after he broke up with me. It just felt hopeless."

"Grief is normal. A lot of people sense a feeling of hopelessness when they experience a loss. You experienced a low, but you didn't get stuck there. You've grown and put some good effort into rebuilding your life." Her words put weight behind what I have been doing lately. I've learned it takes a lot of pieces to put a life back together, and I don't ever want my world to revolve around anyone else again.

We talk about spirit week and how great it felt to be a part of its success. If you had asked me weeks ago to imagine things working out the way they have, I'd never have been able to. When the session comes to a close, Laura asks me one final question. "Do you think you and Gabe will go to prom together?"

I shrug my shoulders, but I can't help the small smile I feel raising my cheeks. I'm not sure I have the guts to ask him, but the more we talk about prom in student council, the more I am feeling excited about going. Maybe it's because I'm getting used to doing things without Brady, or maybe it's because I imagine doing more things with Gabe. Whatever the reason, it shows me how much progress I've made in getting past this whole terrible experience. With a big smile and cheeks that are flushed with a little embarrassment I admit, "Maybe."

twenty-two

AFTER HITTING A little traffic on the way to the Staples Center, Gabe parks in a public lot a block from the arena. I've never been to anything like this and I feel a rush of excitement as the streets fill with other concertgoers and merchants selling souvenirs. Gabe takes my hand when I get out of the truck, and we move along the sidewalk in the current of people.

"Are you hungry?" he asks, leaning in so I can hear his voice over the buzz of the traffic and the angry horns of the impatient drivers. I love the way his warm breath feels against my skin and how comfortable it is to be this close to him.

"Yes. My mom wants to buy our dinner. She gave me money and told me I should insist." We step off the curb along with a large group of teenage girls wearing bright-green T-shirts with giant black Xs on the front.

"Then you can choose where we go." He tugs me to the right, separating us from the mass of people heading toward the concert venue. It's at this exact moment that our time tonight starts feeling like a real date. There's a part of me that can't imagine a more perfect night or a more perfect person to spend it with, but another part is screaming that I am not ready for this yet. Gabe squeezes my hand lightly and stops me, turning so he can look into my eyes. "You okay?"

I can't help but smile, and I feel the negative voice in my head get a little quieter. He makes me happy and being with him like this feels right. "Yeah. I'm good." He looks at me a little suspiciously, then nods his head and leads us to the directory. We decide that the steakhouse would be perfect and make our way over. The tables are set with white cloths and fancy napkins, and the staff is dressed in slacks and button-down shirts.

Gabe pulls my chair out for me and then sits across our small table for two. We both order sodas and when the waitress leaves, he reaches over to my side and takes my hand in his, turning it over so he can rub my palm with his thumb.

"What's going on in your head? I can see that you're

distracted." His eyes move from my palm to my eyes and before he can move them away again I see a hint of worry. My stomach drops and it suddenly becomes a little harder to breathe.

I clear my throat. "There are these moments when I realize that I'm doing things I never thought I'd be doing again. It just hits me. Like when we were crossing the street back there, I was thinking about how excited I am to be here with you and how much this feels like a real first date." His face softens.

"And you're worried about that?" he asks. I nod my head and reach my other hand out to his, squeezing until he looks into my eyes.

"I'm afraid if this turns into something more it will end badly. I love being friends with you and I don't want anything to ruin that."

"I love being friends with you too, but I also want more." He pulls my hands a little closer. "We don't have to rush it. I know you're afraid and I understand where that fear comes from. I can't promise we'll be happy together forever, but I can give you my word that I would never do to you what he did." His words make me smile and I feel myself fall a little in love with him. It's an incredible feeling, almost euphoric. My breath catches as I watch Gabe reach for his menu, completely unaware of what's happening inside me as we sit here.

The waitress returns to the table, but I haven't even glanced at the fine black print of the menu. My eyes are locked on Gabe, and everything else is just noise in the background.

Those bright, multicolored eyes are back on mine and Gabe's lips are pulled up into a crooked smile. I feel like I'm melting. His head tips to the side and his eyes flash to the waitress. They are waiting for me and I shake my head to try to focus on what I'm supposed to be doing. I order the first thing I see and she excuses herself, leaving me alone with him again.

"What are we doing, Gabe?" I ask, needing to know if he really thinks we could give this a try.

He leans forward with his elbows on the table. "Whatever you want." His tone is serious, and his eyes shine bright with hope and honesty. "I'm just waiting for you to lead the way. I know that neither of us is perfect, but I like the way our broken pieces fit together."

I feel a tear slip down my cheek and for the first time in over a month, it's a tear of happiness instead of pain. His hand lifts slowly and wipes it from my face and then his fingers hook beneath my chin and he urges me forward, his lips drifting closer to mine. In the middle of a fancy restaurant, among the clinking of silverware against china, he kisses me. He kisses me like no one is watching, like it's as necessary as breathing, and I kiss him back, because since the first day we met I haven't stopped falling for him. It's a dive and a race, a rush forward into the scary unknown, and I've never looked forward to anything more.

"I love being with you, Gabe. You make me forget all the crazy things that run through my mind. I'm just so afraid to lose this." I chuckle a little. "I even told my sister she's to slap me if I hand over my heart again, and yet here I am with you probably doing exactly what I told her to stop me from doing."

"So then what do you want this to be? And you'll break my heart if you say 'just friends.'" His adorable smile makes my own grow larger. "Friends aren't supposed to kiss each other." He reaches for his water and takes a sip. He hasn't moved out of the space we share over the small table.

"No, I guess they aren't," I tease. "Do we have to give it a label? I'm afraid once we do it will be ruined. Besides, I don't want everyone watching and waiting for us to fail." I take a sip of my water too, as my anxiety begins to build, and I can feel my heart pounding and my hands getting a little shaky as I set the glass back down.

"I don't need a label. That's not what this is about." I feel a wave of relief at his words, that he's not pressing me to define "us." I know he's a great guy and I don't want to lose him, but I also don't want to get lost in him and make the same mistake I made with Brady. I'm hoping when the time is right to make things more serious, I'll know it.

twenty-three

THE LIGHTS DIM as we make our way to our seats. The arena is filling up fast and as the darkness ignites the energy in the room, Gabe tugs me to the front row of the first section. I can see the stage so clearly my amazement makes my smile almost painful. We aren't in the group of screaming girls gathered at the foot of the stage, but we are close enough that I'm going to be able to see the performers' fingers as they play their instruments.

Lights flash up on the stage as the opening act begins to pound out their unique beat, trumpets and drums bellowing out into the crowd, making it impossible to sit still. Every time I look at Gabe, he's watching me, a beautiful smile on his face. He reaches for my hand and when the band clears the stage, he pulls my hand to his mouth and presses a kiss to it.

"Are you having fun?" he asks.

"Yes! I can't believe we're here. I bet my ears are going to be ringing by the time we're finished." I tuck some hair behind my ear and he uses his free hand to do the same to the hair on the other side of my head. His expression tells me that he's having fun just watching me enjoy this so much.

"I'm sure they will, but you'll recover, I promise." He kisses me gently.

"Sometimes the experience is worth the pain." He may not know it, but growing close to him I'm learning the experience of being with him could be worth any pain I might feel over it in the future.

The lights dim again and this time a single large spotlight follows Ed Sheeran out onto the stage. He starts to play, and I'm completely mesmerized by the way his fingers glide so easily over the strings of his guitar. The screens behind him light up with images of colorful toy blocks as he sings of building a Lego house. The words resonate with me, they seem so perfectly suited to my relationship with Gabe. Ed sings of promises of picking up the pieces, mending the broken, and shelter from the storms. The crowd around us sways along to his heartfelt plea to surrender his heart and swap it for his lover's.

Gabe is watching the Legos on the screen building and then breaking apart, morphing into different images. I thought I wouldn't be able to take my eyes off the stage, but now I'm struggling to decide whether I want to watch the performance, or Gabe's reaction to it. His eyes dart over to mine and he cocks a brow before pointing to the brightly colored toys climbing up into the dark sky beyond the screens.

I've been listening to these songs while I run, but nothing compares to hearing them performed live. My heart is soaring and I feel like I'm in on something special, even though there are thousands of people at this concert. It's like nothing I've ever felt before.

The slow strum of his guitar pulls me in as he records the first layer of a song on the loop station. He does this a few times, changing the pace or adding something until finally the song comes together as he steps back and closes his eyes, focusing on playing in harmony with the songs he's just created in front of us. When he steps up to the microphone and sings the first few words of "Kiss Me," I scream along with all the other girls.

Grinning at me, Gabe stands up and pulls me to my feet so that we are facing each other. My body molds to his as one strong arm wraps around my waist and steadies me against him. His other hand is still holding mine and our faces are now inches apart. We rock back and forth, dancing as if the song was written for us, knowing every word. He smiles at me and I don't worry that we are in anyone's way or that the space we are occupying is too small for dancing. Everything wrong is unimportant and the only things I care about are those that bring us together.

When the song finally fades, Gabe's lips press to mine and he pulls my hand in his between us so they are wedged between our hearts. He kisses me and I feel my legs grow weak, my heart swelling so much it's hard to breathe. I let go of his hand so I can wrap my arms around him and his arms cinch tight around my waist, pulling me so close I have to rise up on my toes. He releases me with a kiss to my forehead when the next song begins.

I pray that the concert will never end because I don't think the night could get any better, but when I find myself in the truck with Gabe afterward, sitting in the dark parking lot by the airport near our houses, I know I was wrong. It's perfect. This time we sit inside the cab since it's a little cold out. The music is playing as we recall the performance and watch the planes take off over us.

"Best concert ever!" I yell even though I don't have anything else to compare it to. He laughs and tugs me closer to him on the seat.

"What was your favorite song?"

"There is no way I could pick! Are you kidding? Each one was amazing." I turn my body toward him and watch his eyes dip down to my bare legs. I scoot closer to him and lay my head on his shoulder. His hand moves to my knee, his thumb tracing small circles on the inside of my leg.

A loud plane flies over, silencing our conversation. I rest my hand on his. When the plane is gone, he turns to me and puts his hands lightly around my waist, pulling me onto his lap. It takes a little adjusting, but quickly I'm straddling him, my skirt pushed up enough to allow my legs to fall on either side of his. I love my view from up here, his brilliant eyes shining up at me and his soft lips waiting to meet mine.

"Everly, you look absolutely beautiful tonight." His voice is a rough whisper and he lets his lips lightly brush mine. I feel his warm hands on my hips slipping a little lower, gripping me and sliding me forward to him.

I let my head fall back as he trails kisses down my neck, his hands gliding up to cup my breasts. I move my hips and roll them, loving the low groan that escapes his throat as I rub against him and he rocks his hips up to meet me. My hands keep his lips on my skin, directing him to where I want them the most. The tingle of his touch has me crazy with need.

"Everly," he says with a moan. I try hard to focus my

half-lidded eyes on his face, feeling the way my cheeks are flushed with desire.

"Gabe," I answer with a sly smile, seeing in his face how badly he wants this—needs this like I do. His low chuckle vibrates through my body, sending goose bumps across my skin.

"Tell me you're ready for me to touch you," he whispers, his eyes hazy with desire. He looks straight into my eyes, letting me know he won't push me further than I want. I trail the tip of my tongue along his lower lip and feel him press up against me while pulling me down a little more roughly against him. His eyes close as the pleasure courses through us.

"I'm ready."

His right hand moves from its place on my hip and slides down over my skirt before trailing up my thigh, pushing the soft fabric up with it. When I feel his thumb graze my panties I exhale sharply, tipping my hips up in a silent plea for him to relieve the need that has been building inside of me.

His eyes are on my face, watching as I experience his touch.

I feel empowered on top of him. The confidence I've lost this last month comes pumping back through me with the look in his eyes and the way he seems desperate to touch me. I *am* desirable. I *am* wanted. I *am* needed. And with each touch of his fingers I'm sure I've never felt so good in my entire life. My eyes fly open, staring into his, expressing to him the words I can't seem to form with my mouth. *Please don't stop.*

I close my eyes again and surrender, trusting him completely. I suck in a breath, my heart pounding so fiercely I know he can feel it where my chest touches his. "God, you're incredible," he whispers, kissing my head and holding me tightly to him.

I reach for the button on his jeans but his hand covers mine and stills my movement. I'm surprised and sit back and open my eyes so I can see his face. He smiles at me and slowly shakes his head. "One step at a time, beautiful. I don't want you to wake up to any regrets." He holds me a little longer before he takes me home, insisting I wear his hoodie up to the door so I don't get cold. He doesn't have to insist much; I gladly take it, not daring to tell him that I'll be sleeping in it so I can be wrapped in his warmth and his scent.

twenty-four

I DON'T WAKE up to regrets. My body feels alive with energy and I can't resist putting Gabe's hoodie on over my clothes before leaving for school. I play my music loud on the ride to campus, happy that I can picture Ed singing each word now that I've seen it in person.

As expected, Gabe is already at my locker, leaning against the one beside mine with a shy grin on his face. I want to kiss him, and it's such a powerful feeling that it seems to burst past any apprehension over what other kids will think. I stop in front of him and look into his eyes, loving the way his smile stretches across his handsome face.

"Any regrets, Everly?" he asks playfully, causing my cheeks to feel heated and my own smile to grow.

"Not even one," I whisper. I put a few of my books into my locker while Gabe waits for me. I finally give the door a small push and twist the lock to clear the combo, then turn so I'm facing him again. "Got a second?" Gabe nods and follows me down the hallway to a stairwell that is almost always empty. I give him a sly smile.

That's all it takes. He reaches for me, pulling me close to him and pressing a kiss to my lips. My hands flatten out against his broad chest and I love the rush of adrenaline that courses through my veins. I'm on my tiptoes now, letting his tongue into my mouth and feeling the heat of his body against my own.

He lets go of me and it feels like I'm falling back to earth, even though I'm only lowered about an inch. He gives me one last chaste kiss and then pulls back so I can see his face. "We're about to have an audience." We both hear the sound of feet noisily descending the staircase. "Are you sitting with me at lunch?"

"Yes. I'll meet you here after fourth period." His eyes lift over my shoulder and I know he's worried about me being a topic of conversation at school even more than I already am. I put my hand lightly on the side of his face and his eyes fall down to mine. This time I lean up and capture his lips with my own. He's still at first, not sure what to do, but then his hands find my hips and I can feel him smile against my lips.

The day seems to drag on, but finally the bell rings for lunch. I leave my fourth period class and head for the locker bay, beating him there. I grab the sack lunch I packed with him in mind. There are more cookies than sources of protein and I know that he will have brought two sports drinks since I usually take most of his. It occurs to me that we've already switched a few small parts of our lives from *mine* and *yours* to *ours*. Lunch is ours, this hoodie is ours, and our Tuesday appointments are ours.

When Gabe rounds the corner of the locker bay I can see that something is wrong. His face is serious and he is typing out something on his phone. I watch as he runs his hand up the back of his head like he seems to do when he's nervous or worried.

"What's the matter?" I ask when he stops next to me.

"Maggie has been texting me all morning. It's nonstop and I'm worried. I can't get ahold of my mom or dad and I'm beginning to freak out." I reach for him, wrapping my free arm around his back and peeking at his phone as he sends the message.

"What's she saying?"

"That's just it. She isn't making very much sense. She

says she needs to go running and I told her to wait for me. I don't think she should go alone. She's at the sporting goods store right now buying new running clothes. My parents gave back her access to her bank account, but I think she might be going a little overboard."

I look up into his tired eyes and see the fear that is beginning to build behind them. "Maybe you should go home and check on her. Has she been taking her meds?"

He shakes his head and shrugs his shoulders a little. "I don't know." He tucks his phone into his back pocket, but the worry on his face remains.

The kids around us are clearing out, leaving us in a nearly empty locker bay. "What can I do to help?" I ask, feeling completely useless.

"There's nothing anyone can do. She has to be healthy enough to want to stay that way. Even if we all fight for her, we can't do anything unless she fights for herself." My arms are around him now, his head resting against my shoulder. I hold him like he held me that first time.

I can feel him taking in long breaths, trying hard to remain calm when we both know his world is beginning to spin a little crazy. "Go home, Gabe. Go be with her. She might need you."

"I'm scared." His voice is barely a whisper and his tone and words send goose bumps down my spine and along my arms. I close my eyes and hold him tight, trying hard to express that I won't let him go until he is ready. I nod against his cheek.

"I can go with you."

"I should do this on my own. She's my sister for the rest of my life. I need to get over the fear that her illness is going to take her and I'm going to find her dead." A big breath escapes me. I can't imagine having to be fearful of something like that when it came to my sister.

"Text me. I want to know that you're both okay." I hold him for a minute longer and then he pulls away and his mask of calm is back in place.

"Thank you. I'll text as soon as I can." I walk him to the visitors' gate and watch as he slips through and out to the parking lot. My stomach is in knots and my heart is aching for him.

By the time the student council meeting is called to order after lunch, I have nearly drained my phone battery, constantly refreshing the screen and checking for messages from Gabe. Another rally is scheduled for this Friday to remind students about prom and the formal fashion show that will take place the Monday of prom week. The senior president comes up with the idea that we should all wear prom dresses or suits to the rally to get the other students excited about the evening. I nod my head in agreement and mark everything down on the activities calendar.

I'd never go out and buy a dress for a rally that will only last for a half hour, but I know that Rosie has a beautiful dress she bought last year and then ended up outgrowing before homecoming. It was tragic at the time, but now there is a spare gorgeous dress ready for an occasion just like this.

I pull my phone from my pocket again and try to check it inconspicuously under the table. I hold my breath as a message appears.

GABE: Something's wrong. I don't know what to do. My parents haven't responded to my messages.

I feel my stomach drop and my heart race. My fingers shake as I type out my response.

ME: What's the matter? What's happening?

GABE: She's acting crazy. She cleaned the whole house today and now she's insisting on running off some of her energy. I can't stop her.

I hear the voices in the room around me but my world is shrinking, falling in on me so that all I care about is keeping this lifeline to Gabe. I feel helpless and so scared for him.

ME: What can I do?

GABE: What can I? FUCK she won't stop. I can't understand her. She's just going on and on about random things.

ME: I'm leaving. I'll be there in a few minutes.

I wait for his response but it doesn't come. I finally lift my head to find the meeting over and everyone dispersing to get started on their assigned tasks. Balloons are being blown up and the acrid smell of markers is filling the room as butcher paper is laid on the ground and posters are made.

I grab my bag and shove all of my stuff inside. I look around but don't see Mrs. Cramier, so I swing my bag over my shoulder and vaguely mention to our secretary of sports that I need to head to the office for something. She nods her head and waves me off, too busy talking about what dress she will wear on Friday to notice there isn't a thing I could possibly need from the office right now.

The visitors' gate is locked, of course, but there is no one around as I try the combo a few times. I've watched Gabe do it twice now and I let out a rush of air when the lock springs open. I close the gate and latch the lock again before heading for my car. I call my mom as soon as I am safely inside. When she picks up the line I wait as I hear her saying good-bye to a patient.

"Everly? Is everything okay?" She sounds concerned and I swallow down the fear that is starting to cause bile to rise to my mouth.

"I don't know. I'm fine, but Gabe left school today because his sister was acting weird." My mom knows he has a sister, but I didn't tell her any more about it because it felt like a violation of his trust.

"What do you mean by 'weird'?" She is so calm, which is such a contrast to my beating heart and racing thoughts.

"She's bipolar and she's not very good about taking her meds. Gabe got some alarming texts from her and couldn't reach his parents, so he went home to make sure everything was okay." I grip my steering wheel even though I'm still parked in the school lot.

"He did the right thing. That can be a very tough situation. Has he heard from his parents yet?"

"No. What should we do? I left school and I'm in my car. I want to help him, but I don't know how." I feel the tears sting the backs of my eyes but I force myself to relax now that I have my mom's help.

"Give me Gabe's number. I'm going to call him and get his parents' contact information. He can focus on his sister and I'll worry about trying to get in touch with them. There isn't much that you can do, sweetheart. Maybe just be there for him. Remember you can call 911 if you need to, but it's probably best if she can be convinced to go to her psychiatrist or the hospital on her own. Don't worry, honey, everything will be all right."

I nod my head even though she can't see it and quickly pull the phone from my ear, disconnecting the call and bringing up Gabe's number in my contacts. I send it to her and then a quick text to Gabe.

ME: I called my mom. I'm sorry. She's a doctor and I didn't know what else to do.

GABE: TY running

I stare at his text, a little confused until I realize he is running with Maggie. Of course he wouldn't want her to be alone right now. I turn the key in my ignition, determined to get to him. I head for my house and run upstairs, changing as quickly as I can and lacing up my running shoes. I check for texts from him but there is nothing. My phone begins to ring and my mother's name flashes on the screen.

"Any luck?" I stand up quickly and run back down the stairs and out to my car.

"Not yet. I'm still working on reaching Gabe's parents. He told me he and his sister are near the intersection of Anza and Sepulveda. I told him I'm going to send you to try to get them. Drive carefully."

"I'll be there in two minutes. Thank you, Mom." I toss my phone to the passenger seat and pull the car out, driving quickly to where he might be. I see them as they turn the corner and pull up slowly beside them. They are sweaty and breathing heavily. I can see the fear and worry all over Gabe's face and he shakes his head slowly in defeat.

"Hey, Maggie!" I yell out the window with a smile. She

smiles back at me and waves. "Can I give you a ride?" It's a long shot but I'm willing to try anything.

"I don't need a ride. Isn't it such a beautiful day? I'm out here to feel the heat of God's sun and feel him on my skin. It's great to be so close to him and his creations. Come join us!" She motions for me to get out of the car.

"It's too hot to be running! Why don't you climb in and we can go back to your house and sit on the deck?" My words aren't even all the way out and she's already shaking her head.

"Not today, Everly! Can't you feel it?" She tips her head back and throws her arms out, almost as if she's a worshipper on Sunday morning. I watch Gabe suck in small breaths. He's running out of steam and he stumbles a little when Maggie runs straight into the crosswalk without looking for cars. I pull over and jump out of my car, falling into step with them and tossing Gabe my keys.

"Go find your parents," I whisper, but the volume makes no difference because I don't think Maggie is even listening to us. She is running like she just started, only her drenched clothing giving away the physical strain on her body. Gabe nods at me and then stops, putting his hands on his knees and bending over, gasping for air. I watch him over my shoulder. He stands up and turns around, punching his fist into the air in a show of frustration before screaming obscenities and collapsing forward again. I feel his pain all the way to the deepest part of me.

I reach for the band around my wrist and pull my hair up into a ponytail, quickly wrapping it around and effectively pulling the hair off my neck to keep cool. Maggie turns to face me, a smile spreading across her face.

"Yeah! You decided to join me. Doesn't it feel good? I love this feeling." She seems to bounce a little, and I smile back at her, saving my breath for the run ahead.

I run beside her, feeling the heat of the day beating hard against my face. The perspiration is beading up around my hairline and dripping down my back, soaking into my shirt and the back of my shorts. I keep my breathing steady, letting my feet pound the pavement in step with hers. I'm clenching my hand around my phone, praying that Gabe gets to his parents before my stamina lets me down, or my phone battery dies and I lose my only ability to communicate with the adults trying to help us. We run for what feels like forever—the sidewalks once crowded with students leaving school grow sparse. The traffic picks up, letting me know that people are leaving work and heading home. Still we run on.

The vibration, when it comes, almost goes unnoticed in my swollen, sweaty hand. My body isn't used to running in this heat and I can feel the change in my limbs as they protest the physical exertion. I look down at my phone, feeling a drop of sweat slide down my face before splashing my screen.

GABE: Where are you? My mom had me pick her up and we're leaving our house now.

There's no way I can type without falling so I hold my phone up and snap a photo of the road in front of me. I just hope he recognizes the scenery. I send the picture and clamp my fist back over my phone, careful not to let my pace fall behind Maggie's. She is lost in her own thoughts as we race down the street past a large apartment complex. She's beautiful, even with her hair stuck to her skin and the red, fiery blush of her cheeks from the sun and the physical strain. Her lips curl into a smile for no reason that I can ascertain, and I understand how hard it would be to love her and try to convince her that feeling on top of the world isn't always healthy.

We don't stop even when I notice Maggie starting to show signs of fatigue. I'm already tired, but I'm in this for Gabe and I refuse to let him down. I don't know what drives her to keep moving forward against the bite of our sore muscles and the punishing rub of our shoes against the swollen skin of our feet. We go on and on, and I know that as I run, she flies. She's not here with me right now, her thoughts soaring to a place I could never reach without the aid of some chemical substance. What a miraculous and devastating experience it would be to walk a mile in her shoes. Instead, I run in mine beside her.

I hear the familiar roar of Gabe's truck before I see him on a side street ahead of us. He stops when just the front hood is visible from behind the house on the corner. When he steps out of his truck, he is still in his clothes from earlier, the material hanging from his wet skin. I almost cry—I'm that grateful to see the finish line of this relentless race. I worry that he won't be able to make her stop, but then a woman who can only be their mother steps into sight and I hear Maggie slow her pace, falling behind me as we approach them.

The woman, who so clearly resembles her daughter, quickly shoos tears away from her eyes and motions for Maggie to come to her. I slow down and walk beside Maggie, hoping that this is finally over.

"Maggie, we need to go." Their mother's voice is soft but insistent. Maggie cocks her head to the side and wipes at the sweat before it has a chance to roll into her eyes.

"I'm not going. There's nothing wrong. It's just a little exercise. The doctors say it helps." She's now stopped and I wait with her a few feet from Gabe and their mother. I feel like an outsider who should not be witnessing this tough moment between them. Mrs. Darcy only shakes her head and repeats the same motion for her daughter to come to her.

"Maggie, we need to go," she repeats and now my heart is hanging in the space between us. If she runs or refuses, it will completely shatter. I can't watch Gabe hurt like this. His face seems so pained, his eyes red and swollen.

"They'll just send me home, Mom. I'm fine." Only she doesn't sound fine. She sounds disconnected and unconvincing. Her mother just opens her arms a little wider. Maggie takes a few tentative steps toward her. What happens next destroys a small part of me. She crumbles, her legs bend, and her arms wrap tightly around her own waist. She sobs as she begins to rock on the ground. I move to her and hug her before I even have a chance to think about whether or not it's okay. She quietly sings, "I don't want to go. I don't want to go," over and over, quickly, until I feel my own tears hot against my cheeks.

A soft hand presses comfortingly onto my back and I release Maggie, letting her mother hold her and pull her back to her feet. "Come on, baby," she says warmly. We walk in silence to Gabe's truck and I sit beside him in the front while Maggie's mother embraces her in the backseat. I don't ask where we are going because I already know. We take the quiet back road tucked behind the large hospital and wrap around a private street, stopping when we reach the front of the acute psychiatric hospital.

A tall man with dark hair like Gabe's is waiting on the bench in the front, along with two men in scrubs. All three smile at us as we pull up, and I know immediately that the man in the middle must be Gabe's father. He helps Maggie and her mother out of the back. Then he opens my door as Gabe cuts the engine and slides out on his side. We all stand for a minute next to the truck, everyone aware of what is about to happen but no one ready to get it started.

"I'm sorry," Maggie says, lunging forward to wrap Gabe in her arms. He closes his eyes as he holds on to her, and I would give anything to know what he is thinking. He lifts her feet and spins her in a circle before setting her back down.

"We'll get this. One day we'll get it right." I hear the crack in his voice as he backs away, letting her wipe the tears from her face.

She looks to me next and pulls me into a tight embrace. "Thank you for running with me." She laughs a little through her tears and I do too, embarrassed to be crying in front of so many people I don't know. I nod my head and step back. Maggie turns around and starts to make her way to the front doors of the facility. The men in scrubs walk peacefully beside her and I'm grateful that this is going smoothly.

Gabe's mother catches me off guard, wrapping her arms around me even though I'm sweaty and she's clearly dressed for work. "I can't thank you and your mother enough. I'm afraid to think what would have happened today if Gabe didn't have you." She lets me go slowly, hanging on to my wrists for a second before her husband places his hands on her shoulders.

"Thank you," he says over her head. I smile and nod. He looks to Gabe. "We're going to have to stay here for a little while so we can meet with the doctor and make sure Maggie is settled in. Go on home. We'll call you as soon as we know anything."

We stay where we are until his parents disappear behind the doors at the end of the walkway. They close with a loud clunk, punctuating the separation of Maggie's world from ours. Without a word we climb back into Gabe's truck and drive to his house, where my car is parked.

Gabe pulls up outside but doesn't immediately get out of the truck. Instead he turns to me and says, "Stay with me."

twenty-five

AFTER SENDING A quick text to my mom telling her what's happened, I follow Gabe into his house. My legs are weak from the pounding I put them through as I ran alongside Maggie—by far the longest distance I've ever gone. Gabe is still wearing his workout clothes and I can see the dark contrast of the fabric where it has been soaked with sweat. I run a hand over my hair, feeling the way it tangles in the matted wet strands.

Gabe pulls me down the hallway to his room and into his en suite bathroom. He turns to me and the painful emotional struggle of the day is clearly visible in his eyes, but we are still silent. Today was traumatic for everyone. He toes off his shoes and I follow his lead, kicking mine to the side as our eyes lock. Even with the wear of today on his face, he is still strikingly handsome.

I haven't chanced a glance in the mirror, but I know that I must look horrible. I can feel my clothes sticking to my body. My face still feels hot from exertion and I'm sure it looks at least as worn as his. Knowing all of that, I still reach out slowly, lightly placing my hands on his hips and hesitating before tugging him a little closer to me. He doesn't fight it, allowing his feet to close the distance and my nose to brush lightly next to his.

This kiss feels different from the ones we've shared before. It's like warm honey, sweet and slow, flowing from where our lips have met. His tongue dances with mine, a delicate movement that seems to speak of connection and love. Of course it couldn't be, right? Have we known each other long enough for this to be love? The thrill of falling in that direction has been so fun and innocent, but the thought of actually arriving at the place where I hand over my heart is terrifying. Gabe pulls back and looks into my eyes again and I can see that he feels it too.

He lets go of me for a second and reaches into the shower, twisting the knobs until steam begins to billow out from above the glass doors. We haven't said a thing aloud since stepping into the house, but I feel so connected to him. Maybe it's our souls talking in some way we don't know about, or the fact that we have just been through something so scary that no words could express better what we can see in each other's faces.

The bathroom fills with steam and he steps inside the shower stall fully clothed, reaching for my hand to guide me in beside him. The water falls onto his head and rushes over his closed eyes, falling in beautiful streams from his face. He opens his eyes and I notice the way they are rimmed in red, a reminder that he has been crying. My heart clenches in my chest and I reach up to touch his face, needing to soothe him. I feel my own eyes grow wet with tears as I softly rub my thumb across his cheek, desperate to erase his pain.

His hands are back on my hips, spinning us around so that I am beneath the stream of water. He pulls the band from my hair and then combs his fingers through the tangles, clearing paths for the water to rinse away my sweat. I close my eyes and tilt my head back, wanting the water to wash away the reminder of the fear and despair I felt while running with Maggie. Gabe's hands leave my skin and I tip my head back up, opening my eyes to see where they've gone, missing them already. What I find is Gabe taking in my image slowly, studying the water as it covers my clothes and makes them stick tightly to my body.

My breathing changes with the look on his face, his own heavy breaths giving away his rapid heartbeat and growing desire. His eyes are hot and predatory when they reach mine and I have never felt as needed as I do right now. We stand in the steam and spray of the hot water locked in a world of our own. He seems to be holding back while everything inside me is aching to touch him and give him comfort to push away his pain.

"It wasn't supposed to be like this," he whispers, and I'm already shaking my head. I'm grateful he wants our first time together to be perfect, but where it happens won't change that it was meant to be.

"Maybe it was always meant to be like this." I smile at him. "We've both seen each other's scars, we've both been there when it mattered. I don't think it needs to be flowers and candles. For us it just needs to be real." He hesitates, letting his eyes drift back down over my curves. I step toward him, leaving the stream of water and pressing my soft body against the hardness of his. I close my eyes and squeeze the water from my hair, then twist it over my shoulder.

His hands slip under the hem of my shirt as his warm mouth kisses the delicate skin just under my jaw. I feel the goose bumps tingle across my skin as he slides his hands over my ribs, peeling my wet shirt up my body. He separates his lips from my skin long enough to pull the shirt over my head and then they are back, trailing down to my shoulder as he tenderly undresses me.

The water allows his hands to slip across my skin adoringly, turning on every nerve as he explores my exposed skin. I can feel the slight scratch of his jaw as he sucks on my neck, knowing perfectly how to make my heart beat seemingly just for him. The air escapes my lungs in a rush and I feel a wave of dizziness as longing floods my soul.

I pull his shirt off and then let my hands run along his bare, moist skin. He's warm beneath them and I slide my palms down his neck and across his shoulders before skating them across his pecs and descending to his abs. When my fingers slip beneath his waistband, his mouth stills on my neck, and he looks into my eyes. I can see so many things reflected back at me, and none of them could ever be expressed with words the way he is telling me with one look.

My body feels heated, a hot flush reddening my skin as I listen to his breathing. I feel drunk on him. The world around us is fuzzy and I can't seem to get close enough. I can see the slight redness on his cheeks and the way his eyes are as hooded as my own. The water is growing cooler now as it hits my lower back, making his hands feel hot when he touches me.

"I've got you." His rough voice vibrates in my chest as he wraps an arm around me. He's holding me close, but my arms are wrapped around him too. He's been holding up the world for awhile, but now he has me and I'm not letting him go.

"Gabe." His name slips from my lips, a soft plea to understand I'm here for him. Maybe this isn't the perfect chapter in a fairy tale, but it's perfect for us.

I'm breathing in his breath and he is breathing in mine, making this connection feel deeper than any before. He pulls back slightly so that he can watch my face.

I can see so many things in his beautiful eyes, the way he wants me, the way he needs me, and the way this act of tenderness has managed to push the pain from before aside.

His eyes dip down to my lips a second before he softly kisses me. I feel my heart grow and press almost painfully against the walls of my chest. Sharing this with someone is a huge step, but I know no matter what comes of this thing between Gabe and me, I've never trusted anyone more with my heart.

twenty-six

THE MOST AMAZING feeling of floating keeps us tangled in each other's arms until our breathing is back to normal. I wait for Gabe to step away and leave me, the way Brady always did, but he doesn't. He closes the distance between our mouths and kisses me long and delicately, his tongue lightly meeting mine, our lips, slightly swollen, gently tugging at each other. He slowly sets my leg down, but doesn't make any movement to separate us.

When he finally moves his face away from mine, his eyes look different somehow. I can still see the red outlining them, but the pain seems to be dulled for the moment, replaced with adoration. His hand slides up the side of my face, his fingers moving through my hair as his thumb brushes across my cheek. I can still hear the water running in the background, but it seems so unimportant against the sound of his breath.

He pulls my mouth back to his for one more toe-curling kiss before stepping back from me and pulling me under the stream of water. He steps out of the shower for a second and returns when he's taken care of the condom. The water is almost cold now and we quickly soap our bodies and rinse off before stepping out and grabbing towels. The steam from earlier has all but cleared as we finally emerge into his room.

Gabe tosses me a pair of boxers and a T-shirt before slipping into a pair of workout shorts. The eerie quiet of the house reminds me of the serious reason we are here alone right now. He opens his bedroom door and turns on the light in the hall just outside his room. I feel grateful; suddenly the dark had seemed to roll in around us, bringing with it the emotional darkness of this afternoon. He walks over to me and I feel the lump in my throat return when his sad eyes meet mine.

"Stay with me a little longer?"

We climb into his bed and he tucks his pillow under his head, extending an arm next to him so that I can lie on his chest. I close my eyes when my cheek rests against his warm skin. I can hear his heart beating as his arm wraps around me, hanging on so that I'm tucked as closely to him as possible. His free hand swipes across my forehead, brushing my hair back and smoothing it down until his fingers capture just the tips. He weaves the ends between his fingers.

"How long will she have to stay there?" I ask softly. My head rises with his chest as he inhales in a large breath.

"It depends." I think maybe that is the only answer I'll get, but a few seconds later he continues, "She isn't actively a threat to herself or others like before, so I think maybe just long enough to get her meds back on track and make sure she's stable."

I nod my head against his chest. His fingers, still playing with my hair, pause in their twisting.

"Can I ask you a question?"

"Of course," I answer. "Anything."

"What do you write on that paper you always tuck in your books?"

I'm curious about the shift in our conversation, but I imagine he wants to talk about something other than his sister right now.

"Homework my therapist gives me. Sometimes she has me keep a log of my negative thoughts and asks me to replace them with more helpful ones." I bring my hand up to his chest and absently draw circles with my fingers against his skin. "We've been working on my 'staircase of fear.'" His hand resumes its weaving.

"What's that all about?" His hand at my back splays out across my skin, the warmth quickly seeping into me and giving me comfort.

"It's a progression, like a staircase, of little scary moments that build up to the worst one. I had to pick my biggest fear and work backward." I wonder if he'll think it's stupid. I haven't told anyone else about the assignment because it seemed too private to share.

"Will you tell me what your fears are?" He presses a kiss to the top of my head.

"I feel a little silly now. Some of them don't really seem that scary anymore. It's more like each is a step on the way to closure and letting go. Let's see, should I start from the lowest step or the highest?" I have them memorized. I feel him shrug below me and I rest my palm flat against his chest. "I'll start from the bottom and work my way up. Please keep in mind that the steps might seem ridiculous to you, but at the time I wrote them they were more about grieving what could have been than actual fear. I was just afraid to live the moments because I knew they would hurt and no amount of preparing seemed to make any difference."

"You could never be ridiculous." His tone is serious and I appreciate that. I nod and snuggle up to him, moving my face slightly closer to his neck.

"Invitation to prom, which will lead to an awkward family photo experience, which will then lead to the cheesy professional prom portraits that I had always pictured taking with Brady." I shake my head a little and he tugs on a strand of my hair, which makes me laugh.

"Continue."

I take a big breath. "I'll have to slow dance with someone else at my senior prom. I know it seems silly, but I dreamed of the perfect ending to my senior year, and Brady and me being together is how I had pictured it. If I dance with someone else then that's it, the night will slip by and be lost to us forever. That leads to my biggest fear. I was afraid of how bad it will hurt to leave prom without him." I give him a slight smile. "But somehow that staircase doesn't seem like a staircase of fear any longer, just a necessary path on the road to outgrowing those childish dreams."

He and I haven't talked seriously about prom. We laughed about the promposals and he now knows the fear I had built up around not going with Brady, but he doesn't know that I've been thinking about it in an entirely different way lately. At night before I fall asleep I think about what it might be like to be there with Gabe. I wonder what it might be like if *he* asked me. In the back of my mind I remember the agreement I made with Laura that I'd ask someone myself if

I didn't get invited soon, but tonight it just doesn't feel like the right time.

It's so quiet I can hear my own heartbeat. I wonder if my words have hurt him. We just had sex and I know I'm falling hard and fast for him, but I don't know how he feels about me now, or what it might feel like for him to hear me talk about someone else. "I'm sorry," I say quickly. His hand slips under my chin and he turns my face to his, kissing my lips chastely.

"I asked, and you answered honestly. I don't expect you to wipe him from your memory. You guys were together a long time, and I know you have the memories to go with that history. I'm not hoping to take his place—I'm too selfish for that. I want a place of my own in your life." He smiles a cute smile and then kisses me again before laying his head back and resuming playing with the ends of my hair.

"Can I ask *you* something?" I wriggle my cheek against his chest until I'm comfortable again, glad to be looking away while I ask this question.

"Sure."

"What's in the notebook you take with you to counseling?"

"Are you sure you want to know? You can't unhear the answer." I don't hesitate to nod my head. I want to know everything about him that he's willing to share with me. He curls a strand of my hair around his fingers.

"I'm working on a response to Maggie's suicide letter." His words pierce straight through my heart and my throat tightens.

"Why are you doing that?" I slide my hand over his chest tenderly, wanting him to know how much I care about this journey he's on.

"My therapist thought it might be helpful." His answer is honest and neutral and his body remains relaxed.

"Is it?"

Once again I feel his shoulders shrug beneath me. "I haven't finished. I go back and forth between being angry with her and being scared and hurt. The irony is that the letter seems to swing from one mood to the other, kind of like her illness. My therapist said that her doctors and I would have to decide whether or not I ever give the finished letter to her, but getting my thoughts out should help the way I feel about it." His voice cracks and I wrap my arm around him and hold tight.

I watch his deep intake of breath and the slow way he blows it out like I do when I'm trying to stay in control of my emotions. "I'm so scared. I'm afraid she'll kill herself. I'm afraid I'll be the one who finds her again." The catch in his chest lets me know he's losing the battle to keep his emotions calm. I feel my own tears warm my cheeks and drip onto his chest, but I say nothing, knowing he needs to tell this to someone.

"Damn it," he says more to himself than to me. "I'm afraid she *won't* kill herself—that she'll just live the rest of her life miserable in order to make us all happy. I'm afraid I *won't* be the one to find her—maybe my mom will and she won't be able to handle it." My heart breaks for him. "I'm just so fucking scared of it all." He sniffs and his hand leaves my hair to wipe away the tears he has failed to keep inside. I crawl up to him, kissing his forehead and pulling him close. I hold him like this, both of us on our sides, his face pressed into my chest as his arms wrap around my waist.

"It's okay," I whisper. "It might get rough and scary again, but right now she's safe, Gabe, and that means there is a chance the doctors can get through to her. Maybe this will be the time she listens. Maybe this will be the time she wants to stay healthy." I rub my hand softly down his back.

I rest my cheek against the top of his head and feel the warm tears slide down my face and onto his pillow. His pain is so deep I can feel it myself, and I would give anything to know what else to say that might help him feel better. What he's going through is so much bigger than any of my fears, his heartbreak so much deeper. I want to tell him I'd do anything for him and that he can count on me to be a constant part of his life even if his sister experiences her ups and downs. Instead, I just hold him. I hold him like it's what I was meant to do and like I could do it forever, because I know that I could.

It could be just a few minutes, or maybe even as long as a few hours, but sometime in the darkness he finally succumbs to sleep and it's with his calm, even breaths that I begin to feel peace myself. I close my eyes and hold him tight until I fall asleep beside him.

twenty-seven

IT WAS WELL after midnight when Gabe's parents finished up at the hospital and came home. Very little was said
about what had happened, all of us exhausted from the
ordeal. Mrs. Darcy assured me that Maggie was doing much
better and was not angry with any of us, but that didn't alle-
viate the guilt I felt for my part in it. Getting her into treat-
ment was the right thing, but it must have felt like everyone
was against her.

My own parents let me climb the stairs to my room and
crawl into bed with just a soft "Goodnight" and no further
explanation. When I opened my eyes in the morning to the

sound of my alarm, my mom was at my door, telling me to go back to sleep and that I could get to school in time for third period. I worried about what Gabe might think if he didn't see me at my locker in the morning so I texted him to let him know I would be there later, but he didn't respond.

When my alarm goes off for the second time, I awake with anxiety already swirling in my gut. It feels like a rough sea tossing during a storm, and I have to use every tool Laura has given me to calm it down enough to climb out of my bed. I'm not anxious for myself, I am torn up over the heartache I saw in Gabe's eyes. I check my phone for messages, but Gabe hasn't responded to the last text I sent.

After getting ready for the day, I drive to school feeling a mix of anticipation and dread. I want to find Gabe. I make a quick stop at the office to grab my tardy slip and then I rush to class. I'm disappointed when he isn't waiting by my locker at lunch. By the end of the day that disappointment has morphed into worry. Even though I am supposed to be spending sixth period helping with prom preparation in the student activities office, I spend most of the time check-ing my phone to see if he's texted. No matter how hard I try to focus on the task at hand, creating posters and locking down the plans for Friday's rally, my mind keeps pushing my thoughts back to him. By the time the final bell rings, my stomach has twisted into a terrible knot and I have the heavy feeling of dread sitting low in my gut. I haven't heard from Gabe all day and at this point no amount of deep breathing or reframing my thoughts is helping the sinking feeling that he's not okay.

I skip the last trip to my locker and rush out past the front of the school. My thumb is flying over the screen of my phone, typing out a text message to Gabe, when I hear the noise around me suddenly go quiet. In horror movies, you know something bad is going to happen when the music gets louder and every movement the character makes seems amplified. But today, as I absently race to my car, it's when the soundtrack to my day halts that I realize something is wrong. I was in such a rush to get to my car that I didn't even realize I was walking through cheer practice. I've wandered into Elle's territory, carelessly stomping right through the middle of the girls, all of whom have stopped talking.

I wait for the fear to hit me. I've actively avoided this moment for weeks, carefully planning my exits so I don't have to walk this gauntlet. My eyes meet Elle's and I watch as her face becomes rigid with discomfort. There is a new feeling that surfaces within my heart as I keep my eyes locked on hers. For the first time since this whole mess started, I feel pity for her.

It would have been so easy to lob emotional grenades in her direction. I know just as much about her as she knows about me. I too could have spilled secrets that would've hurt her personally as well as socially. I've thought about it, and if I'm honest, I've come very close to lowering myself to her level. It's been a rough journey, but I know now, in my heart, I'm the bigger person. I've managed to climb out of all the rubble she's caused to fall on me by breaking down and exploding my friendships and reputation. This is where the pity creeps in. I can already see the regret hidden poorly behind her expression. It's going to eat her up inside, and I know that because I know her. She hasn't always been a villain, which makes seeing so much darkness in her hard since I've also seen so much light.

As I stand before her, the girls to her left jump down from their stunt and all eyes turn to take in what is happening on the small stretch of grass between the school and the parking lot. It's a moment like a standoff in an old western movie. The air between us grows thick with tension, and the other girls watch with curiosity, wondering who will draw first and who will be around in the end to walk away.

There are so many things I want to say to Elle, but as they enter my head in rapid succession, I realize that nothing I can say is going to change who she is or what she's done. I can still read her, the way her lip twitches when she's about to lie, the big intake of air when she's trying to stay calm, and the small crease that lines her forehead when she's not sure what to do next.

I don't hide from her any longer. I take a few direct steps toward her and she shifts her weight nervously, making me wonder if her heart feels heavy from all the damage she's caused. "Hi, Elle." I have been avoiding this conversation for far too long and now I regret the time I've spent these last few weeks trying to come up with some way to tell her how badly her actions hurt me. I know now that I shouldn't have to spell it out, it's obvious to everyone, and that includes her. She knows exactly what she's done to our friendship and my heart.

"Can I talk to you for a minute?" she asks cautiously. "You're not returning my calls or texts." I feel sorry for her. I can see now that she's hurting too, but I can't take any responsibility for that pain. I held up my end of our friendship and that allows me to hold my chin up when I shake my head no.

"There's nothing you can say, Elle."

"I can say I'm sorry," she practically whispers.

"I wish that would fix it." My throat grows tight with emotion, but it's not hurt that I'm feeling, it's closure. Our friendship is over. "Even if I forgive you, I'll never trust you again. What's left of a friendship when there's no trust?"

Her face crumples and I watch her cry for the first time since she made the choice that broke my heart. "Nothing," she answers. I nod my head and realize that it's her turn to grieve. We all lost something through this experience.

Rosie steps to the front of the group and gives me a hug. She's been my cheerleader through this entire friendship breakup. I feel the relief radiating off her as her warm arms squeeze me tightly. She smiles sadly at me when she steps back and there is a clear change in the group dynamic. It's as if many of them have just been waiting for me to be brave enough to face Elle and make a decision about where she stands in my life. Now that the war is over, no one will feel pressure to choose a side. I've finally freed myself from this self-imposed exile.

I've had someone be a true friend to me these last weeks, and what Elle has offered me in the past as friendship now pales in comparison to my time with Gabe. I'm also closer to Angie, and a few of the other girls I worked with to plan the senior prank. I don't need her. "It was nice to see everyone," I say. "I've got to run. Enjoy practice." With that, I turn and head to the parking lot, trying hard to contain the smile I feel screaming to be set free.

I slip into my car and close my eyes. I expand my lungs, drawing in a deep breath and releasing it. I feel the slight shake in my hands, the aftermath of the adrenaline that helped propel me through that awkward situation. In the quiet safety of my car thoughts of Gabe begin to swirl in my head. When I leave the parking lot I head for his house instead of mine. There is a nagging thought at the back of my mind that maybe he wasn't at school because something happened with Maggie.

His driveway is empty when I pull up in front of his house. I only realize how much I was hoping he'd be here when it becomes clear that he's not. It suddenly seems like there are miles between us. I thought last night had intensified our relationship, but maybe I'm the only one who feels that way. It's a strong reminder that we both have demons we're fighting, and while I'm close to getting past the events that have turned my world upside down, Gabe is fighting a demon that will never go away. He will forever be terrified of what could be with his sister.

I drive around for a little while, not ready to go home. I end up at a small playground my mom used to take me to when I was younger, and decide to park beneath a large tree at the edge of the lot. I grab my backpack and head over to a shady area of grass beneath a tall tree. I spend the next two hours there, finishing my homework and watching the kids play in the sand while their mothers talk to each other.

I have a few things I need to handle that I fell behind on when I left student council early yesterday and tuned out sixth period today. I dig my phone out of my backpack and dial Angie. She picks up on the third ring. "Hey, Everly."

"Hi, Angie. I'm sorry I haven't been much help the last few days. I was wondering if you have a few minutes to talk about the rally tomorrow." I might not feel like working on anything right now, but I've learned over the past few weeks that I can't withdraw from everything just because things might not be going my way.

"Of course."

"Can you catch me up on where we are so far? I sort of spaced out today." Having a few hours to myself at the park has helped to clear my head. I want to know what's going on with Gabe, but for now there is nothing I can do about it. I'll just have to wait for him to reach out.

"We sent out the voting cards for each homeroom so that they can vote for the best promposal. Mrs. Cramier and Coach Carter will count them up tomorrow morning and will have Mr. Eager make the slide that will be shown behind you when you make the announcement." I hear the sound of a zipper on her side of the line followed by pages turning. "Also we voted on a playlist for when the students walk in and when they walk out. I'll take a picture and send it to you so you'll know when it's your cue to start the rally."

"Thanks, Angie. And thank you for all your help these last few weeks. I couldn't have done any of this without you."

"It's been fun. I knew you would be great at secretary of activities. It's been a blast working with you on everything."

Her words mean a lot to me and I feel my lips curl up into a smile. I did it. I managed to fulfill my duty as secretary of activities and put together ideas that everyone liked. It's a great feeling.

"Thanks again. See you tomorrow."

"You're welcome. See you then." The line disconnects and I tuck my phone back in my bag when I see there are no other messages or texts. When it starts to turn from day to evening, the visitors to the playground begin to pack up and I follow their lead, tucking my books into my backpack. My phone chimes inside my pocket. I swipe my finger across the screen and a message appears, and I feel relief for the first time all day.

GABE: Come watch the planes with me.

twenty-eight

THE BACK ROAD that leads to the parking lot where I know Gabe will be is crowded with workers leaving the factories that line this area of the city. I haven't even texted Gabe back, too anxious to get to him as quickly as possible. When I finally pull my car into the nearly empty lot, I feel a wave of relief when I see his truck backed into his usual spot. I should have known earlier that he would be here.

He doesn't move when I step up to the back of his truck. Instead, he keeps his eyes trained on the sky. "Hey," I say in greeting.

"Hi," he answers. I watch him for a minute, taking in his

tired eyes and the defeated look on his face. I lean against the lowered tailgate, following his gaze. I feel the shift of the vehicle when he climbs to the edge and rests on a knee, extending his hand to help me up.

My soul has been starving for his touch all day, and it is with great relief and happiness that I wrap my fingers around his and allow him to lift me high enough to get my knees onto the cold, hard metal beneath us. I watch as he climbs back to his folded blanket, but his eyes don't return to the sky above, they look deep into mine as he raises his arm in an invitation for me to lie on his chest.

I curl into him, closing my eyes and letting his warmth surround me. There is nothing more important in this moment than just being with Gabe. All of my attention is on the way his strong muscles feel beneath me. I find it strange that he doesn't smell of the chlorine I have grown to associate with him. His hand rests on the top of my head before stroking downward, capturing the ends of my hair between his fingers much like he did last night.

"I'm sorry," he says gently. His eyes return to the sky above us. His jaw seems tight and his eyes seem haunted.

"It's okay." I let my hand slide across his chest, wrapping my arm around him and pulling myself closer. He shakes his head.

"It's not. I've been working on a few things. I needed a

little time to get my thoughts straight. It wasn't cool to ignore your texts, so thank you for forgiving me." I'm not sure what to say, so I say nothing. "I want to share with you one of the things I've been working on." His hand slips through my hair again but doesn't trail to the ends. Instead, his fingers move lightly across my jaw and his lips meet mine ever so softly.

Directly over us a plane leaps into the darkening sky, creating a loud and powerful roar as it passes. Gabe breaks our kiss and slowly moves his fingers from beneath my chin. With his eyes still on mine, he reaches beside him and brings his familiar notebook to his chest. He's inviting me to read what he's written and I feel both honored and terrified.

"Are you sure?" I ask as my fingers move along the cover. He gives me a tight smile and a little nod of his head. I move so that I'm on my stomach, my upper body supported by my elbows. When I flip the cover open I can see that some of the lined pages have been ripped out. Remnants of scribbled writing and smudged black ink are visible on several strips of paper that have not been fully removed. I let the tips of my fingers glide over the letters, the imprints they have made gripping my heart because I know how difficult each attempt at writing this note must have been.

When I finally come to the page that has been left intact, he reaches into his pocket and sets a folded and worn piece of paper on top of it. "You should probably read this first."

His voice is a deep monotone. I swallow past the lump in my throat and feel myself bite down a little too hard on my bottom lip in an attempt to keep my emotions at bay. His thumb presses into the soft skin above my chin and tugs lightly down, springing the trapped lip free. He swipes his rough fingertip along it before moving his hand so he can tuck it behind his head.

It feels so important, this note I know he must have read a million times. The paper has become a little fuzzy in a few places where it's been worn and is beginning to show its age. The writing on it is frantic, but the curling tilt of the lettering easily gives away its female author. My heart nearly stops when I see that it is addressed directly to Gabe. No wonder he's carried the weight of her attempt so heavily across his shoulders. My eyes feel the sting of tears before they have even taken in the message.

My Dearest Gabriel

I'm just so tired. The doctor has said that there is no cure for this roller coaster I'm riding. At the top there's so much joy. The sun feels like it's always shining, even in the darkness, and my soul feels full and peaceful. I know now that while I'm living at the top you are waiting breathlessly for me to plummet back to the ground. That's exactly what I do. The fall is quick and unimaginable, only to end with this unbearable misery that can't be described with any words I've ever found.

I know you must be thinking that I was insane when I wrote this, but let me assure you this letter is being written in a moment of clarity. A few days ago I was so low that I couldn't even get out of bed. Today I awoke with a clearer mind and knew that I needed to carry this out while I could because there is no promise that tomorrow I won't find myself that low again.

I love you and ask that you forgive me for this. Trust me, your life will be better—brighter, even, without me. I will always be a cancer to our family and it will only end when I'm gone. Imagine a life where you don't have to worry about me ever again! Please tell Mom and Dad I love them. No one could have stopped me, so don't ever doubt that you all did what you could do. I've lived my life feeling very loved and taken care of. The battle is completely inside me and I just can't do this anymore.

I love you,
Maggie

I close my eyes and let the tears fall down my cheeks. Gabe brushes the wetness from my face. We don't say anything; we just sit in the quiet for a minute as I fold the note up the way it was when he handed it to me. When Maggie's words are tucked neatly away, he takes the note from me and puts it back into his pocket. I wonder if it has always been there. I'm watching his face when his eyes dip down to the notebook below me, his response to that heartbreaking good-bye.

Maggie,

Your diagnosis hit us all hard but never changed the way I feel about having you as a sister. You have always been a shining star, so bright that I felt the only thing I could do was run after your light. I will be happy to do that for the rest of our lives. You are mistaken when you say that I'm waiting at the bottom of your inescapable roller coaster. If you'd only look hard enough you'd see that I'm sitting right next to you. We go up together—we fall together. If you kill yourself, you will be killing a part of me.

You ask me to forgive you for taking your life. It's taken me a long time and a lot of therapy, but I will do this for you. I'll do anything for you, but I need you to know that forgiving you isn't a one-time event. I'd have to forgive you for every moment in my life that I'd want you there for, and since you're my big sister, it's going to be a lot of forgiveness. I'd have to forgive you when I graduate (and that's a big accomplishment since school isn't as easy for me as it is for you), on my wedding day, at the birth of my children, and every time I'd reach for the phone to talk about something with you. It would be millions of moments that would be robbed of complete happiness because you weren't there.

You tell me that there is nothing more I could have done, but that won't stop my mind from trying to solve the puzzle. I would wonder, could I have tried harder? Listened more? Come home a little earlier? This would be the cancer you'd leave behind—the tiny seed of doubt that would grow roots and take hold in my mind and heart.

Don't give up, Maggie! I can't promise you'll always be at the top of the roller coaster, but I can promise that if you kill yourself you will be giving up any chance of rising above the misery of the bottom.

It's because I love you that I will try to forgive. I will try my hardest every day if your decision is to leave us, but that effort will be so much more exhausting than the effort it takes to sit beside you when you're feeling low. The happy memories of you in my life will quickly be outnumbered by the days I'd feel a painful void without you.

So what do you say, Maggie? Let's strap ourselves into this roller coaster from hell and ride it until we've memorized the turns and conquered each drop in the track. Let's ride it every day until we own it.

I love you in this life and beyond,
Gabe

twenty-nine

THE SKY IS dark above us as I close Gabe's notebook and roll onto my back, hugging it tightly to me. "I think you're braver than I am. Your letter is beautiful and somehow perfect, even in such a terrible situation. I think she's asking too much of you when she wants you to be okay if she decides to kill herself. I've been thinking about Maggie a lot lately, and no matter how I look at it, I just can't get to a place where I'd be able to tell her she could give up. I know I wouldn't be able to do that for my sister if she asked." I turn my face to him so I can look into those beautifully colored eyes of his.

"I've looked at it from every angle I can think of," he

responds. "It's not that I'd be okay based on some great understanding of her situation. My acceptance comes from having no other option. I can fight her on this, and I still will, but as I pulled up and saw the two of you running your miserable race, I realized I have absolutely no say in whether or not she ends her life.

"I can talk to her about it, beg her, make the act itself difficult, but in the end she'll make her choice with or without my support and maybe even in spite of it. My struggle to stop her became a reason for her wanting to do it. She is literally watching me become crazy with her illness and it's killing her. You don't think you could do it for your sister, but you might think differently if you were in my shoes." He leans forward and presses a soft kiss to my forehead.

The roar of an engine pierces the air again and we both look up at the bright lights of the plane streaking across the sky overhead. I rest my hand on his stomach and he immediately puts his warm palm on top of it. "My therapist told me the other day that one idea about heaven is that in that space we decide what we need to learn here on earth. We enter into contracts with other souls and then return here to carry out those heavenly contracts. I don't know if I believe it, but there is something peaceful about the idea. Maybe Maggie and I are carrying out a contract of selflessness." He draws in a deep breath and blows it out, giving my hand a few small pats. "Or maybe she's my lesson in letting go."

I push myself up so I can give him a reassuring kiss on the cheek. "What's our contract then?" I ask, letting my eyes fall from his and trail slowly down his face.

A smile tugs at the corners of his mouth. He laces his fingers through mine and dips his face closer to me before whispering, "Unconditional love, of course." His warm lips meet mine tentatively and I close my eyes, feeling his words seep into my skin. He loves me. I realize I love him too, and would love him until my heart was black and blue. There is something about the way he is with me—his little gestures, his perfectly crafted words—that has made me fall for him and continue to fall deeper than I ever thought possible. He fills my heart so completely it's practically bursting and yet each day there is something more.

"I kind of like that idea of life and death," I muse. "It makes everything that feels so pointless here hold some sort of cosmic value. Brady dumped me and the world just kept spinning as if it didn't even care that I was falling apart. Maybe it was something we had already worked out before we were even born. He was *my* lesson in letting go—"

"And you were his lesson in not letting something good slip away. He might not see that yet, but I can. I've watched you heal—I've seen you lick your wounds and nurse them back to health, the layer of protection growing thicker with scar tissue. With his own actions against you, he's given you armor against him. He's created the scars that protect your heart from him."

"What if you decide one day that I'm not enough?" I hate to sound so needy, but it's one wound I can't seem to figure out how to treat. That fear lurks in the back of my mind no matter how much work I put into pushing it out. I pull my bottom lip between my teeth as I wait for his answer. His warm palm slides across my cheek, caressing my face and directing my gaze to his.

"That's easy, Everly. You'll always be enough." I start to shake my head, but he laughs a little and holds me still. "But if someday I wake up insane enough to question that, I'll remember that it was never about you or me, it's about us. If it feels deficient, then we'll just have to become more. Together." I can't help the small blush that warms my cheeks. I know he sees it when he rubs a thumb across the pink skin.

I move up onto my elbow so I can look down at his face. I can see the honesty and the small crinkles of amusement around his eyes. My hair is falling down around us and he moves both hands into it, combing it with his fingers off our faces. That's when the last little ache I feel for my life with Brady vanishes—shaken from my heart by the quick flutters Gabe causes. His smile falls for a minute as he watches my face. If I didn't know better I would think he'd read that thought, snatching it right from my mind. His fingers tighten as he pulls my lips to his.

My hand is twisted in his hoodie now and I breathe him in as our mouths softly dance together. I smile against his lips and he returns the gesture, brushing my hair back and holding it at the nape of my neck as his tongue slowly enters my mouth, seeking further connection.

I feel myself shiver from the cool night air and of course from the way he gets my blood pumping. He chuckles and reaches into the far corner of the truck bed for another blanket that's folded there. He shakes it out and pulls it over us as I kiss his neck and jaw. Once the blanket is settled, his hand slides up my side, gently wrapping around the curve of my ribs and pulling me against him. I slide my leg over his and feel the heat of his thigh between my legs.

Another plane flies over us, heading off to some unknown destination, the only other company we have in this empty parking lot. Slowly Gabe pushes against me, guiding me onto my back beneath him. He settles between my legs, my knees bending to cradle him to me. It is delicate and smooth, the way our bodies move together, arching and reaching for what we need and connecting in a way that feels much deeper than just physical.

I close my eyes at the scratch of his face against mine as he dips his chin and kisses my neck. I tip my head back and offer him more skin, pushing my fingers through his hair and holding him close. His hand slips beneath my shirt and runs up my back until his fingers are gripping my bra strap. He pulls his head away from me to look into my eyes and I can see the question in them. I nod my head and let my own fingers slip beneath the hem of his hoodie and shirt.

The clasp is released and his hand unhurriedly moves to my chest, gently exploring. When my fingers grow more urgent, he lifts away quickly and tugs both his shirt and hoodie over his head. His skin is hot beneath them and I run my hands down the hard plane of his chest and then lower, to his clenched stomach muscles. He takes a second to look around before exposing my skin. The cool night air makes goose bumps rush across my skin, but he answers the cool caress with his own heat as he covers my body protectively with his. His lips move determinedly toward my ear and the small sensitive spot just below my lobe.

His hand slides down my side, over my hip, and to my zipper. The next few minutes are a dance of soft kisses and gentle touches. The items keeping us apart removed one at a time. He moves his body to my side and turns me, tucking himself behind me so that he can hold me close.

His lips are on the back of my neck, his hands twisting my hair out of his way. I feel heat in the wake of the trail he is kissing along my spine. Gabe reaches for the blanket and pulls it over our heads, creating a small pocket of space in which we can be together in our own little world, unseen.

I should be anxious but I'm not. I should be overthinking every step I'm taking getting closer to this amazing guy, but it's impossible when all I can think about is how incredible it feels to be accepted for every part of who I am. And maybe being under this blanket in the back of his truck isn't really protecting us from the weight of the outside world, but for tonight, it's enough—we're enough.

thirty

GABE HELD ME close until it was time for me to go home. It seemed like I was floating, resting in the peace that comes from being held by someone strong and honest. He kissed my lips lovingly before tucking me into my car and telling me he wouldn't be at school tomorrow. He told me he was working on something with his dad, and I didn't question him about it. He might need a few more days to get his life back to where it was before Maggie returned to the hospital.

I'm wide awake now, my heart still beating rapidly from the excitement of spending time with Gabe. I'm happy again and I know that there are risks in any relationship, but I'm starting to trust Gabe with my heart. I'm looking forward to my next appointment with Laura so I can share with her all the progress I've made this past week. I also want to ask her for some insight into what living with bipolar disorder might be like and if there is any way I can be helpful to Maggie.

When I get home I head up to my room to work on a few assignments that are due next week. Even though I'm trying to focus on the work in front of me, thoughts are swirling around in my head, and instead of pushing them away or trying to avoid them, I take a minute to consider them so I can use the tools I've learned for facing my anxiety head on. I'm jotting down my questions for Laura and working out some of my fears and negative thoughts with the technique she taught me.

Situation: Gabe loves me.
Feelings: Joy, elation, fear, anxiety
Unhelpful Thoughts: He doesn't know me very well yet
*   and when he does, I won't be enough.*
Alternative Thoughts: He doesn't know all of me but he
*   loves me already. Laura says the second time falling*
*   in love is even easier since I already know how to*
*   build a relationship and express my wants and needs.*

I feel tears pooling in my eyes when I write the next alternative thought that I never believed would sound true: *I am okay on my own and will survive no matter what.*

The rest of the night before I fall asleep I go over what I'll be announcing at the rally tomorrow. I'm nervous about speaking in front of the entire student body, but the anxiety I have felt at the last few rallies was far less than at the beginning of the school year. It's another intense area of my life I have faced head on and conquered. I think about my goal to ask someone to prom by Monday. I haven't let Laura down yet, but the window to invite Gabe is rapidly closing, and I still haven't found the courage to bring it up. If he wanted to go wouldn't he have already invited me? Asking Gabe to prom would be the first time I've ever asked a boy out, and I'm not sure if I would be able to say the right things when I'm alone with him and my nerves.

I text him as I slip into my bed for the night, mustering everything I have to set up a time to ask if he'll escort me to prom.

ME: I miss you already. Can you meet up tomorrow evening?

His response doesn't come right away and I lie in my bed reflecting back on how everything between us started. I've come so far in the past month, and the overwhelming feeling of gratitude warms my chest and brings a lump to my throat. Gabe has been the light shining down brightly on the place I'm standing, allowing me to see that while the path I was on with Brady has come to an end, there are so many other new and exciting paths I could travel.

GABE: I miss you, too. I'm still working on that thing with my dad. I'd love to get together tomorrow evening. I'd like to take you to dinner and a movie if you're up for it.

ME: Sure. That sounds fun. See you tomorrow.

I don't have the courage to ask him in an over-the-top promposal, even though lately I'd have to admit the idea of a big romantic invitation is sounding better and better. I close my eyes and start to drift off to sleep, planning the route I'll take in the morning after lacing up my running shoes. Bit by bit my old life is coming back to me.

Now it's Friday morning and I'm regretting pushing myself so hard running this morning. It felt so good to have my energy back and to clear my mind while pounding the pavement, but now I'm definitely feeling the consequences of my enthusiasm. My feet protest being thrust at an unhealthy angle into my four-inch heels, and I wobble for a minute before remembering how to walk elegantly in them instead of like a baby calf.

Rosie's dress fits me a little snugger than I'm used to, but I still wasn't about to ask my parents to buy me a dress for a thirty-minute rally. The sleek, bright-blue fabric hugs every curve, dipping low in the front and again in the back, requiring a very uncomfortable bra that feels like it isn't doing much in the way of support. The sequins along the bodice catch the light and cast a twinkling show on the wall around me. I smile with the recognition that the pink tile in this bathroom might not be so dreadful after all. The giggles and excited conversations of the other female members of the student council getting ready around me add to warm feelings of happiness. "Come here, Everly!" Angie squeals as she holds up her phone.

"How many more selfies are you going to take?" I tease, putting my arm around her shoulders and making a face as she takes the picture.

"Just a few more. I can't believe our senior year is almost over," she says, scrolling through the last few photos she took. I peek over her shoulder to see the pictures of us buying the tricycles for the tricycle race and then a large group shot of all the seniors who dressed up for our Seriously Seniors day. "I can't believe we are pulling this off," she says with a sigh.

"It's amazing, isn't it?"

A few of the other girls crowd in to watch as Angie swipes through her album. "I think the tricycle race was my favorite," she says as a picture of Garrett Smith, a linebacker on the football team, tucked onto the tiny trike flashes on the screen. We all giggle with the memory of his head-to-toe riding gear complete with a helmet and motorcycle boots. When the pictures come to a stop, Angie turns and gives me a big hug. "I'm going to miss doing this with you."

"I'm going to miss it too. You have to be in student government at USC," I tell her as I move back over to the mirror hanging above the sinks.

"I'm looking forward to it," she answers, "and I hope you consider it at UCLA. You've done a great job this year. We were a good team." She moves beside me to look in the mirror.

My makeup is a little more dramatic than usual, but I didn't go overboard since I'll have to continue wearing it for the rest of the school day. I've twisted my hair in a Hollywood roll at the nape of my neck and secured a few curls along the top. I brush my bangs to the side, out of my eyes, and pucker my already tinted lips so I can apply a faint hint of gloss. Standing back, I take a long look in the mirror, scrutinizing my reflection. The blotchy remnants of shed tears have long since left my face and I no longer have dark circles beneath my eyes. Instead, they stare back at me brightly, a hint of excitement reflected in them.

In twenty minutes the bell will ring and the students will begin to file into our large gym and pack themselves into the bleachers. With my dress on and my makeup finished,

I leave the bathroom and head over to the gym. I stayed up late last night making sure I had memorized all the important information I'm supposed to announce today. The only thing that will be a surprise to me is who won the free limo ride, because it's tradition that only the teachers know until the moment it is revealed to all students. There is nothing else left to do on my end, so I direct a few of the underclassmen in securing the balloons.

A pair of slender arms wrap around me from behind, and my sister kisses my cheek. The cheer squad will be performing a routine and she looks absolutely beautiful in her crisp uniform. "You look so stunning!" she screeches into my ear, and I spin around and hug her. The bell sounds in the gym and she pulls away, blowing me a kiss as she returns to the squad at the front of the room.

I'm used to being anxious before the rallies start, but today there is the added pressure of not tripping over my heels. I take my place at the podium and watch as the student body pushes through the doorway and spills into the bleachers. The music is playing now and a few students are dancing and clapping in their seats as they wait for the rally to start. I can't help but smile at the wave of excitement that warms me from the top of my head to the tips of my toes. I even let free the giggle that has pushed its way up my throat.

I'm doing this. I'm standing up here for the prom rally and my heart is not breaking. The acknowledgment of victory is sweet.

With a nod from the activities director, I switch on my microphone and welcome the students. "Hello, everyone! I hope you're all ready to get pumped up for prom." I wait for the enthusiastic roar of the students to die down before continuing. As I scan the crowd of students, my eyes land on Brady. He no longer makes my heart pound or even hurt. I smile at him and he smiles back. We survived this. I've grown and changed in so many ways. I'm free. I let my eyes take in the happy crowd once more before introducing the events of today.

"We're going to start by announcing the winner of the free limo ride. We saw a lot of epic invitations these last few weeks, and I know everyone is anxious to find out who took this year's title." People shout out the names of their favorites as Brett, the secretary of music and our drum major, steps forward in his suit and taps his drumsticks on the old wooden podium, creating a drumroll.

We wanted to do things a little differently this year, and the plan is that when I turn around and point to the large white screen, the names of the winners will appear. I wait for the screaming and chanting to build, and when the noise is almost deafening I turn around and point. To my surprise, the lights shut down, casting the entire gym in darkness.

My heart races as I silently pray for the tech to fix the problem before the students become restless. When I look to Angie for reassurance, she smiles and points above her to the big screen, drawing my eyes back to it just as the image of a toy truck constructed out of Legos appears. I feel my brows draw together as it dawns on me that the truck looks remarkably like Gabe's. I watch in awe as a small Lego plane takes off over the truck and the sound of a jet engine echoes through the gym as a soundtrack to the movie.

A Lego man beckons the viewer forward before the camera pans wider, allowing another small Lego figure to be seen. I know it's supposed to be me immediately, and I cover my mouth with my hands, tears welling up in my eyes. The unmistakable sound of Ed Sheeran's "Thinking Out Loud" begins to play as the boy figure takes the plastic hand of the girl's, leading her to the edge of the screen, where a large staircase of toy bricks rises into the sky.

The little man releases her hand and takes a few steps upward, turning and beckoning her to follow. She shakes her head, but takes one small step closer to the first stair. With this, the little man lifts his eyebrows up and down, causing laughter to break out around me. I'd almost forgotten I wasn't the only person watching. Still, I can't take my eyes off the colorful images projected on the screen. Finally the female figure takes a few steps upward, pausing on the step below the man. A line from the song mentions people falling in love with just the touch of a hand, and the boy figure reaches out and grasps the girl's, pulling her up beside him and dipping her back in time with the music. A collective sigh emanates from the female audience members and my lips twitch with the need to laugh and cry all at once.

As I stand there watching this amazing testament to what we've done together, I know that not one other person in the audience will understand exactly what Gabe is showing me in this video. I have no idea how he's managed to pull it off, but if he never does another thing for me, this will be enough. The song urges the woman to take the man into her arms and kiss him under the stars as the tiny Gabe figure walks beside the tiny Everly, hand in hand, and they make their way to the top of the stairs. When they reach the last step he sweeps her off her feet and into his arms. I can't fight it any longer and a hot tear slips quickly down my cheek as I watch the toys jump from the highest step in each other's arms. The screen goes black and the lights in the gym come on one panel at a time as Gabe appears just inside the front doors of the room.

I stand motionless as he smiles shyly at me. He's wearing a tux and carrying a bouquet of multiple colors, orange and brown notably absent. When he reaches me, he takes the microphone from my hand and kisses me quickly on the cheek. My legs feel weak beneath me and I want to wrap my arms around him and tell him how much this has meant to me. He takes a step back and drops to a knee, handing me the bouquet and then reaching for my free hand to hold in his.

The entire gym erupts in cheers, and my chest shakes with laughter and pure joy as he clears his throat and waits for everyone to settle down. Within a few seconds the gym is silent, everyone waiting on his words as he looks up at me with those amazing eyes.

"Once upon a time I finally got to talk to my crush, the most beautiful girl I'd ever seen, in the most unlikely of places. She was trying to find herself again and needed to convince her heart that it still mattered. And I had to let go of the expectations that only I could save someone in order to hold on to this amazing girl with both arms. Now we've reached the part of our story where she has to decide which way it will go from here. So tell me, beautiful girl, will you go to prom with me and let this story end happily Everly after?"

I nod my head and the noise of the crowd rising to their

feet and cheering drowns out the answer as it leaves my mouth. Gabe stands up and I wrap my arms around him as he scoops me up and off my feet. I rain kisses all over him, the joy of this moment almost overwhelming. I move my lips to his ear and tell him the words I was afraid I'd never be strong enough to say again: "I love you, Gabe."

acknowledgments

IT WOULD BE impossible to include everyone who played a part in making this story come to life. Over the years so many stories have touched my heart, and so many tears have been shed in my office over broken hearts, inescapable roller coasters, unrequited love, and, of course, loss. While always personal, sometimes the pain felt was universal. If you have ever trusted me to hear your story as a friend or therapist, thank you.

I'D LIKE TO thank my family for being supportive during this process. It couldn't have been easy to see me come home from a day at the office and sit down to a night at the computer. You guys loved me and gave me the time to follow this dream and share this story. I love you all so much. I hope you are as proud of it as I am.

THANK YOU TO all the family who live outside my house who stepped up to offer support and encouragement. Many of you were the first to read this story and offer feedback. You always asked for the latest news and celebrated each success with me, making it that much sweeter.

JAIME ANGELL, I'M not even sure where to begin thanking you. I will forever be grateful to the universe for giving me a chair in your English class. Today I consider you one of my most treasured friends. When I came to you years ago with the idea of entering a writing contest, you never once made me feel like I couldn't do it. You gave me your free time to support my effort, and with you in my corner I believed I could win—and I did. Since then you have supported me in both careers and outside of them as well. Thank you, my friend.

CHRISTINA ZELLER, I'M thanking you in the back of this story because you did something for me that warmed my heart. You took an interest in my story, read it with enthusiasm, and insisted you take me out to celebrate my book deal. You told me women don't always do enough of that for each other, and you were right. So I'm thanking you for being a great friend and fellow woman. You rock. Our boys are awesome, and we will always be fun room moms even if we pull things together last minute. That's just how we work best.

THANK YOU, CHRISTINE Witthohn, for believing in me. I can't wait to celebrate many more successes with you in the future. I love being a part of your Book Cents family. Without your guidance and hard work on my behalf, this would not have happened. I feel very lucky for the opportunity to be represented by you.

A SPECIAL THANK-YOU to Catherine Wallace and the entire team at HarperTeen for seeing something in Everly and Gabe's story. It's been an amazing experience! I'm looking forward to continuing to work with you and share more stories of loss, love, friendship, and healing.

I HAVE TO give a shout-out to Jo Watson. You have become my friend over the last few years since starting this crazy journey together. I can't wait to see where it takes us. You're a brilliant author and a magnificent friend. I know when I need support you're just a few clicks away with your adorable accent and brightly colored hair and shoes. Thank you.